The Wetherbys

G. Clifton Wisler

The Wetherbys

WHEELER
PUBLISHING, INC.
ROCKLAND, MA

★ AN AMERICAN COMPANY ★

Published in Large Print by arrangement with The Ballantine Publishing
Group, a division of Random House, Inc., in the United States and
Canada.

Wheeler Large Print Book Series.

Set in 16 pt Plantin.

Library of Congress Cataloging-in-Publication Data

Wisler, G. Clifton.
  The Wetherbys / G. Clifton Wisler.
    p. (large print) cm.(Wheeler large print book series)
  ISBN 1-56895-835-8 (softcover)
  1. Frontier and pioneer life—Texas—Fiction. 2. Teenage boys—Texas—
Fiction. 3. Brothers—Texas—Fiction. 4. Orphans—Texas—Fiction.
5. Texas—Fiction. 6. Large type books. I. Title. II. Series

[PS3573.I877 W4   2000]
813'.54—dc21   99-059454
                                                                    CIP

For my father,
Charles Clifton Wisler, Jr.,
who had the good sense
to bring me to Texas

1

Nothing's ever quite what you expect it will be, Jake Wetherby thought as he guided his grandfather's razor across his chin. The times he'd looked forward to shaving! Now it was just another nuisance, something to slow the morning.

"It's not Sunday, is it?" his brother Jericho asked as he blinked sleep from his fifteen-year-old eyes.

"Tuesday, I think," Jake answered as he dipped the razor in the shallow water of the washbasin and shook off the yellow-brown hairs that sprouted amidst the white-gray shaving soap.

"Getting awful pretty for an ordinary day," Jericho remarked as he pulled an oversize nightshirt over his bony shoulders and stumbled over to a pile of discarded clothes. "Chin's pure shiny!" he added as he fished out a pair of overalls. "Like Baby Joe's."

"Nothing like British steel to hold an edge!" Jake boasted, turning the razor over so that it caught the sunlight seeping in through the room's single window.

"Figure to go to town today?" Jericho asked as he studied his older brother. "Or are you trying to impress the hogs?"

"Got a job of work to do for the colonel," Jake explained as he ran the razor across his left cheek. He frowned as he gazed at the razor. There still weren't all that many whiskers to erase. Even at eighteen, he couldn't boast much of a beard. It was the Fitch influence. His mother's folk were on the fair side, straw-blond and late-growing.

"You sure you're Joe Wetherby's boy?" Chris Anders from the farm upstream had asked only yesterday. "Imagine, big bull of a man like that siring runts! No, sir, I'd never figure his boys to run on the small side."

Jake had gritted his teeth and ridden on past the tall Swede without so much as a sideward glance. If it had been a boy saying those words, he would have paid for the remarks with loose teeth and a swollen eye.

"I guess you'll be seeing Miss Miranda, then," Jericho said, sidling over next to Jake and gazing in the mirror. "Won't be long before I sharpen up that razor's twin and use it myself."

"Could be," Jake said as he cut away the heavier growth above his upper lip. "I see some fuzz there."

"Amy Anders says I should grow myself a mustache."

"Does, does she?"

"It'd make me look older, don't you think?"

"Might, at that," Jake said, painting a stripe of soap over his brother's lip.

"Trouble is, you can hardly even see the hairs," Jericho grumbled. "It's the Fitch curse. Pa says he was hairy as a black bear when he was fifteen!"

"You're not Pa, Jer," Jake said as he splashed water onto his face. "Be glad of it, too. You got more of Ma's blood in you, and that's a better bargain all-around."

2

"Pa's not so bad, Jake."

"Was him brought us to Texas, wasn't it?" Jake grumbled. "Him and his dreaming. Killed Ma."

"She was sick all along," Jericho argued. "Grieving for her dead twins. And for Jeremiah. I'm as much to fault for that as anybody."

"You didn't hold him under the water, Jer, nor push him into the river."

"Didn't save him, either."

"Hard to do when you can't swim, little brother."

"Should've learned."

"Let me take another look here," Jake said, pulling Jericho over and probing his shoulders. "Yes, sir, I believe I notice a hump growing here. The weight of the world. Sure must be tough carrying it around with you!"

"That's not funny," Jericho grumbled as he wriggled loose.

"Nope, and neither's you carrying on so!" Jake growled. "You weren't even ten when Jeremiah went and drowned. And I'm hanged if I'll pass the morning listening to you heaping the hurt onto yourself. Boys drown in rivers, you know. Little Charley Collins went and managed to do it in Spring Creek, and the water wasn't even rising. Now you go rouse Jordy and Josh. We've got chores waiting, and they won't get done with them asleep or you moaning either one!"

Jericho looked up with something approaching relief in his eyes. He then skipped out the door.

"He's got the makings, Lord," Jake said,

gazing out the window at a brilliant amber sun painting scarlet streaks through the morning clouds. He might have watched it a bit if the floor hadn't shaken. A shoe bounced off the wall, and voices barked.

"Go away and leave us be!" thirteen-year-old Jordy cried.

"Go away!" Josh added in his higher-pitched eleven-year-old whine.

Jake banged twice on the wall, and silence settled over them. There was no arguing with Jake, and by the time he stepped out the door onto the sheltered porch that divided the boys' half of the dog-run cabin from the other, larger rooms occupied by their father, stepmother, and baby brother, Jericho had managed to collect Jordy and Josh.

"We know," Josh said, shaking his head. "Pigs and chickens."

"Pigs and chickens," Jake agreed, waving the younger boys off. "Fresh water, Jer."

"You chopping, Jake?" Jericho asked as he grabbed a bucket and took a step toward the well. "Shame to raise a sweat with you all prettied up and all."

"Figure to take myself a bath at the creek," Jake explained, laughing as Jericho screwed his face into a scowl. "Wouldn't hurt you to do likewise. Might help your chances with Amy Anders."

"Don't you know that circuit preacher near killed Harvey Lindale baptizing him last week!" Jericho exclaimed. "Water's sure death after August."

"Better to be dead than to smell dead," Jake

said, laughing as he grabbed the big double-bitted ax. "Where women are concerned anyway."

"Hope Miss Miranda appreciates the sacrifice," Jericho said, grinning.

"She generally does," Jake answered as he headed for the chopping block. He left his brothers to their chores as he split lengths of bois d'arc and hackberry logs into stove wood. The better oak and willow wood was always saved for winter. As he raised the heavy ax in his arms and drove it deep into logs, he felt raw power. Sure, he wasn't tall yet, and there was no bulk to his middle, but his arms and shoulders held iron.

"There's more to being a man than growing chin whiskers," his grandpa had said plenty of times. "Meet your obligations, and look men straight in the eye. That's what's called for."

Jake missed the old man. All any of them had to remember him were the two razors, and Grandpa Wetherby had cleverly given those to Jericho.

"Grandpa said to pass this on to you when the need came along," Jericho had explained just before they'd celebrated their first Texas Christmas. "I guess he figured it would wait for your birthday, but the truth is, you're looking downright shaggy."

The twin razors had forged a bond that went well beyond any that blood could have made. Once their sister, Jane Mary, had taken a husband and moved to town, Jake and Jericho had moved into her room together.

"You could have that room to yourself,

son," Joe Wetherby had told Jake. "You're of an age to have some privacy."

"So's Jer," Jake had answered. "He's not so much trouble, after all."

There were times when Jake had reconsidered, but in a pinch, Jericho was reliable. And Jer needed time away from the little boys. There was too much of Jeremiah in their faces.

"You chopping or studying the grain of the wood?" Joe Wetherby growled from the porch.

"Chopping," Jake said, turning back to the work at hand.

"Your ma's ready for that wood!" Joe barked.

"I'll be right along with it," Jake said. And she's not my ma, he added silently.

He struck a hackberry log with such force that splinters flew a dozen feet away, stinging little Josh as he returned from feeding the chickens.

"Hey, Jake!" the boy cried, skipping away. "Don't have to murder those logs, do you?"

"Rather me murder a little brother?" Jake replied.

"No, keep after the log," Josh said, grinning as he danced away from a second shower of splinters.

"Hurry it along!" Joe shouted, and Jake resumed his chopping. Shortly he'd converted five fair-size logs into slivers suitable for the big cast-iron stove. Josh and Jordy raced over to help carry the wood inside, and Jake gave each a good-natured poke in the ribs.

"I never remember you two so skinny when Ma was cooking," Jake grumbled.

"Ah, Betsy cooks fair enough, Jake," Jordy insisted. "She says it's 'cause all the growing's going into my feet."

"Well, that's possible," Jake admitted, gazing at Jordy's dirty toes. The boy was just about all leg now, with a body and arms added on like an afterthought.

"Boys!" Joe shouted, and the three of them hurried on. Each deposited his armful of stove wood in the box beside the stove and scrubbed hands and face in a small basin of hot water.

"You shaved this morning, Jake," his step-mother observed as he stepped around her and sat beside Jericho at the table.

"I do it now and then," Jake muttered, avoiding her smiling eyes. Betsy Randolph hadn't been as old as Jake was now when she'd married his father. She still wasn't much more than a wisp of a girl. Her high-handed rule of the kitchen had driven off Jane Mary, and Jake himself vowed to head out on his own at the first opportunity. If it weren't for his brothers...

"I believe he's got his eye on some girl," Betsy said as she cracked eggs into a greased skillet.

"Miranda Duncan," Jordy said, giggling.

"The colonel's daughter?" Joe asked. "He'll match her with some rich banker or maybe a lawyer."

"Joe, you know better than most it isn't the father who makes the match," Betsy said, laughing.

"She's awful fancy, Jake," Josh observed. "Keeps busy at the station, minding the freight business and tending all those travelers."

"Wouldn't need to do so much if she had a husband," Betsy noted.

"Husband?" Joe asked, laughing loudly. "Boy's not half-grown! How tall are you now, Jacob Henry? Five-foot-six stretched heel to head?"

"Taller'n that," Jake said, glaring at his father.

"Takes after the Fitches," Joe muttered. "I was six feet tall when I was Jericho's age and—"

"Hairy as a bear," Betsy said, shaking her head. "We've all heard that, Joe. I suspect the boys have, too, more often than they care to. I think Miranda Duncan's a fine young woman, pretty as a peach, and well-read by all accounts."

"Books," Joe said, gazing contemptuously at a shelf of volumes Jane Mary had left behind for her brothers. "Never heard how one got a field plowed or a barn built."

"Ma favored learning," Jake argued.

"Never got her anywhere but buried," Joe replied.

That was your doing, Jake thought. His brothers stirred uneasily as Joe Wetherby half rose in his chair. Jake swallowed the words and stared at the floorboards. Shortly Betsy had breakfast ready.

"Joe, would you say grace for us this morning?" she asked as she placed two platters on the table.

"Lord," Joe said, pausing while the boys bowed their heads respectfully, "bless this food to the nourishment of our bodies. Give us rain to fill the creek and temperate weather to renew our spirits. Look after our loved ones here and elsewhere. Amen."

"Amen," the others whispered solemnly.

Joe Wetherby then spooned scrambled eggs onto his plate, set two slices of bacon to one side, and passed the platters along to his left. The boys took their portions, leaving the final measure to Betsy. They ate silently, as was the current custom. Betsy considered it a poor waste of food and time to jabber away while feeding oneself, and it was one rule Joe enforced with an iron hand. Only when Joe himself had emptied his plate, and Betsy had set off to tend her baby, did Jordy venture to speak.

"I hear there's a big horse auction next week in McKinney," Jordy said. "I sure would like to have myself a saddle horse. I'm just about the only boy hereabouts without one."

"They say you can buy yourself a rough-broke mustang for ten dollars," Jericho noted.

"You got ten dollars, Jordan?" Joe asked.

"No, sir," the boy answered. "I thought maybe you—"

"I work hard for the cash I put by," Joe stormed. "We scarcely took in enough corn to do for our own needs."

"We got the peaches in, Pa," Jordy argued.

"Your ma's not got 'em bottled yet," Joe complained. "And what we sold didn't buy you shoes. I figure they're more important."

"Jake could shoot a deer," Josh suggested. "Make us moccasins like—"

"I won't have my sons attend Sunday meeting dressed like wild savages!" Joe declared. "There'll be no more talk of horses."

"Colonel Duncan might have a mount or two he'd let go cheap, Pa," Jake said, scowling at his brothers' crushed spirits. "They really do have a long way to walk to school, especially with winter coming."

"No farther than it has been," Joe argued

"I'd pay for the ponies myself," Jake insisted"

"If you've got so much money filling your pockets you don't know what to do with it, might be you'd care to pay for your keep."

"I do chores, Pa," Jake pointed out.

"Guess that does balance out eggs and bacon," Joe admitted, "but there's the roof over your head. Clothes."

"Make me out a bill, Pa," Jake growled. "Then maybe we'll discuss wages."

"Maybe we should," Joe agreed. "You're always rushing off to do this and that. I could use your help myself."

"Corn's in, Pa," Jake observed. "I picked my share of peaches, too. Who was it dug the new well, by the way? Mended the team's harness? Split shingles and patched the roof?"

"I expect a man to do his share," Joe said. "Just now Sam Chandler and I're building a dam up at his place. Aim to build a gristmill so we don't lose a third of our crop to that bandit Herman Halle. Be some work, and we'd welcome the help."

"The farms hereabouts won't support two mills," Jake said, frowning. "All you'll manage is to kill Halle's business, too."

"He could be right about that, Pa," Jericho added.

"I'll shed no tears for that German," Joe insisted. "People will come to our mill because they trust us. It's closer, too, and before long the country to the north will draw settlers."

"Pa, if you dam Spring Creek, what will we do for water?" Jake asked. "The Selwyns aren't going to like that, either. Nobody downstream will. And what will happen if we hit a dry spell? A mill's no good without a pond. It's just another fool's dream, staking your hopes on some scheme. What happened to the fortune you were going to make with the toll bridge?"

"If we'd had a wet spring, it would have paid for itself," Joe argued.

"Instead the creek went dry, and people laughed. Then when it did rain, it washed that pile of logs right along downstream."

"It will be different this time."

"Sure, Pa," Jake muttered, dropping his napkin beside his plate and rising.

"Jacob Henry, sit down," Joe commanded. "I don't recall excusing anybody."

"Pa, the boys need to head for school, and I'm due at the colonel's. Order Baby Joe around, why don't you? He's too small to notice."

"Jake!" Joe shouted.

"Let him go," Betsy urged as she entered the room with the baby resting on her shoulder. "You said yourself he's a man."

11

"So long as he's under my roof—"

"Don't run Jake off, too," Josh pleaded, gripping his father's hand. "He doesn't mean anything."

Jake didn't hear his father's reply. He was already outside, stepping off the porch and hurrying along to the barn. Shortly he'd saddled Maizy, his speckled corn-colored mare, and was riding north.

2

Jake rode north until he was out of sight of the house. Then he stopped and slipped out of his clothes. The water was cold, and too shallow for a real bath, but he figured Miranda Duncan would appreciate the effort. Once he'd washed the dust and sweat off, he scrambled up the bank and rubbed himself dry. His flesh turned to goose bumps as a sharp October wind blew up out of the north, and he threw on a pair of clean overalls in record time.

"Best appreciate this, Miranda," he said as he shook himself out of a shiver. "It's not every Collin County man that would bother to get himself scrubbed just to see you!"

Jake remounted Maizy and continued riding north and west along the winding stream bed of Spring Creek. It had never been a raging river, but August heat and autumn drought had shrunk it to no more than a wet nuisance. In places there was still water, but a man didn't need to ride more than twenty yards before he found a spot he could splash across. A boy of ten with a running start could jump clear over it without even winding himself.

"And Pa thinks he can dam this and make a mill pond?" Jake asked the yellowing willows. Another man might have devoted the autumn to clearing some acreage for spring planting. Frank Selwyn, who had the farm downstream, had ridden off with his brother-in-law and rounded up fifty maverick longhorns. His family would have beef to eat that winter!

"Texas has all a man could ask for," Colonel Duncan was fond of saying. "Beef on the hoof. Horses eager to accept his rope. Wood and water if he has a nose to find 'em, and all the vexation necessary to turn him to God."

Joe Wetherby would have agreed with that last part, but only that. Being Tennessee-reared, he knew chickens and hogs. Cows were for milking, though, and horses pulled plows.

"It's not his fault," Jake's mother had said shortly before her death. "He expected better land. An easier time. He's fought his battles, Jacob Henry. They've worn him down."

"Then why'd he come to Texas?" Jake had asked.

"For you boys," she'd answered. "And to get away from the graveyard."

Jericho wasn't the only one haunted by little Jeremiah's ghost, and the twins, who hadn't done much more than whimper before dying, bore heavily on her. In the end there'd been too much sadness, Jake supposed.

"That's why he married Betsy," Jericho often argued. "She's so bright and sunny."

"Young, too," Jake had observed.

"Yeah, there's that," Jer admitted with a grin.

Maybe that was why Jake couldn't abide his stepmother. She was so full of life, while Mary Elizabeth Wetherby, the rightful mistress of the house, lay on a lonely hill overlooking a bend in Spring Creek.

The wind stirred suddenly, and Jake felt an eerie sensation on his bare shoulder. It was as if his mother was offering a comforting hand. He straightened the overall strap and glanced backward. Her grave wasn't quite in view, but he envisioned it anyway.

"I'm all right, Ma," he whispered. "Getting along toward tall, some say."

There were some inches yet to go, he suspected, but there was no hurrying such things. It was like waiting for the corn to ripen. Staring at the stalks didn't help.

Jake passed the wooden stake marking the northern boundary of the farm. Up ahead he smelled cook smoke rising from the Anders chimney. Mrs. Anders was famous for flapjacks and berry preserves, and Jake was known to happen along in time to wrangle an invitation. Not that one breakfast wasn't enough, but there was plenty of space to add pounds on his scarecrow frame.

That morning, he skirted the Anders farm

instead. He did spy Amy and her little brother Christian scooping water out of the shallow creek. They exchanged waves, and Jake wondered what a kid with Jericho's reddish-blond hair and light coloring and Amy's flaxen hair and freckles would look like. The poor child would be downright invisible!

Upstream another mile lay the Chandler place. You couldn't call it a farm. Sam Chandler had yet to plow one row. If there was a man around with more schemes and dreams than Joe Wetherby, it was surely Sam Chandler. Some said he'd left Carolina with five thousand dollars and gone through most of it the first season. Now he got by on bank drafts sent by his wife's father.

"You know, he's a fair blacksmith," Colonel Duncan once told Jake. "I always send the teamsters over to him when they pull in with a bad wheel, or when somebody needs a horse shod. Can't imagine why a man with a trade is forever throwing money away on foolish notions."

Jake found the colonel's disdain particularly funny since John Duncan was famous for half-baked enterprises. Miranda said he owned acreage in twelve counties and was still buying up land script good for sections out west in Comanche country. He ran cattle into towns not a good day's ride from prowling herds of longhorns, and he sold mustangs at country auctions where most men were already horse-poor to begin with.

"Yeah, there's smarter things a man can do," the colonel told Jake once. "But I always walk away with cash money, Jake. Texas provides, you see. I trust in her and the good Lord. They've done fine by me so far."

Then, too, the colonel had Miranda to watch his money. She was nothing if not practical, and if there was a way to squeeze thirty cents out of a quarter, she'd do it.

"It's her Scots' blood," the colonel once remarked.

Miranda told a different story. She'd gone without enough to know it was no road to walk. Better to have cash salted away against future need than to find yourself short.

There was a generous side to her, too. For a couple of years she had sent dresses along to Jane Mary, saying they were in unclaimed trunks and there was no point in them going to waste. After a time Jake recognized a dress or two, though.

"Wetherbys don't take charity, Miranda," Jake had complained bitterly. "You wore that dress yourself not two months back."

"Well," she'd answered nervously, "I'm not above borrowing a dress from an unclaimed trunk myself."

It was a lie, and they both knew it. She'd sewn one of those dresses herself. But Jane Mary enjoyed something new from time to time, and dress fabric wasn't one of Joe Wetherby's priorities.

Lately there had been different parcels to take south. School slates and boys' shoes. Baby things. A string tie so Jordy wouldn't feel awkward when he sang in the boys' choir at Sunday meeting.

"It bothers you, taking these things, doesn't it?" she had asked only last week.

"It troubles me I have to," he had answered. "I'm not used to needing help."

"I don't have brothers, you know, Jake. It's what draws Pa to you, I suspect. Don't hate us for seeing the need and wanting to help."

"I can do a lot of things, Miranda Duncan," he'd said, grinning. "Hating you's not one of 'em."

Now, nudging the mare into a trot, Jake said, "Come on, Maizy. She'll be wondering what's happened to me. I promised I'd beat the nine o'clock stage, remember?"

The horse snorted a reply, and Jake urged her into a gallop. Soon he swung westward and rode on across the broken ground toward the Preston road. Duncan Station stood just beyond on a spring-fed branch of White Rock Creek. When he got there, he saw the stage-coach had already arrived. Stable boys were swapping out the horses, and Miranda was occupied with the passengers. Even so, she managed a scowl for his late arrival.

"Sorry," he called, noticing how her auburn hair framed her cream-colored face. It was the cool blue of her eyes that warned of trouble.

"Help with the horses," she barked. "I've got breakfast to cook."

He nodded and turned reluctantly to where a pair of young black men were laboring to free four exhausted horses from their harness.

"Don't mind her," the elder, a sad-eyed giant named Nathaniel, said. "Got herself scairt by a copperhead this morning!"

"Any normal gal'd be dead of the fright," the other stable boy, a round-faced fifteen-year-old named Jefferson, declared. "Proper lady'd faint straight away."

"Miz Miranda went inside, fetched her daddy's Colt, and blew that copperhead's head on toward Preston," Nathaniel boasted. "I reckon, knowing her, we'll probably have copperhead stew for supper, too."

"Want not, waste not," Jake said. "Or is it the other way around?"

"Anyhow, you leave us to take care of these horses, Jake Wetherby," Nathaniel declared. "Get yourself into some other mischief. Colonel Duncan expects us to tend to the horses our own selves."

"Figure it's all right if I tie Maizy up by the trough and let her drink?" Jake said.

"You sure ain't looking for my permission," Nathaniel grumbled. "No place of mine to say."

"Go ahead," Jefferson said, laughing at his older companion. "When did the colonel ever say no to you anyhow?"

Jake laughed and led the mare to the trough. Maizy dipped her head onto his shoulder, and he gave her head a scratch. Then he tied off the reins and left her to enjoy a drink.

Duncan Station appeared as large as Austin or San Antonio on an 1855 Texas map, but there was nothing to impress a stranger about the place. The colonel had added two rooms to the back of a modest two-story frame house— a small warehouse that doubled as freight office, and a second room that served as dining room

18

and saloon. Occasionally he hired out two upstairs rooms, but only to the well-bred. Others slept in the stables back of a large corral. There were two privies, an icehouse, and a little cabin where the stable boys lived.

"You can't expect much so close to Dallas," Miranda was explaining to a weary woman passenger when Jake stepped into the dining room. "Now in Dallas you'll find they've got a real fine hotel."

"I dearly hope so," the woman said, washing the road dust from her face. "This journey is simply more than I bargained for. If Horace had warned me, I would have remained in St. Louis."

"Texas can be a disappointment all right, ma'am," Jerry Platt, the driver, observed. "More dust than adventure."

"Well, I would say we've experienced our portion of adventure, too," the woman complained. "Comanches!"

"Comanches?" Jake asked, growing cold. "Where? When?"

"Don't get your dander all up, Jake," Jerry said, laughing. "Was two Chickasaw boys swimming up at Preston."

"They were bare-boned naked!" the woman exclaimed.

"Most people hereabouts swim that way," Jerry observed with a grin. "When we pass the boys' home on the Trinity, best lower the shade, ma'am."

"Oh, she's safe this time of year," Miranda declared. "It's too cold now for swimming. Bathing, even."

She stared at Jake with an amused grin. He knew his hair was still wet, and she would have noticed his clean-shaven chin.

"It's true," Jake assured the woman. "Only a downright fool would go to the trouble."

"To bathe?" she asked. "Don't you Texans know about tubs?"

"Sure," Jake said, grinning. "You put lard in 'em, don't you, Miranda?"

Jerry Platt eyed the female passenger's considerable girth and turned to conceal an equally wide grin. Miranda scowled. Two men sipping corn liquor at a nearby table laughed right away, though.

"Lard, huh?" one asked. "Sounds right to me, don't it to you, Miz Lassiter?"

Miranda silenced them with a frown and led Mrs. Lassiter to an unoccupied table.

"Pa's waiting in the office," she told Jake. "I've got breakfast to make."

"Yes'm," Jake said, giving her hand a slight touch as she rushed past.

"I could manage something for you, too," she offered. "Pan steak and eggs?"

"I could eat," Jake replied.

"Then don't let Pa bend your ear. It won't be more than a few minutes."

"Do my best, Miranda," Jake promised.

He slipped around the bar and opened the narrow door that connected the dining room with the office. There, amidst stacks of trunks and boxed supplies, stood the heavy oak desk where Colonel John Duncan sat.

"Jacob Henry, you're late," the colonel observed.

"I'm sorry, Colonel," Jake said, dropping his eyes.

"Bathed and shaved, huh?" he asked, laughing. "And I'll wager Miranda never said a word about it."

"Some women are hard to please," Jake observed.

"Bet it lands you a breakfast steak, son. Maybe corn fritters, too."

"Be worth it, then."

"Things all right at home?"

"Yes, sir," Jake said, sliding into an empty chair on the far side of the desk. "Why do you ask?"

"Sam Chandler says he and your pa intend building a mill. Wondered where Joe could come by the money. Hasn't struck gold, has he?"

"No, sir," Jake answered with a frown.

"Don't let him borrow off you, Jake. It's a fool's plan, and you shouldn't encourage it. Spring Creek won't support a mill, and the folks downstream won't abide a dam."

"I told him as much," Jake confessed.

"Well, there's no telling some people," Colonel Duncan said, laughing. "Nobody's ever been able to argue me out of anything. If I had half the money I've thrown away on this and that, I'd be sitting in my mansion, smoking Virginia cigars and laughing about it right now."

"Yes, sir," Jake said, matching the colonel's grin. "You said you might have something for me to do."

"I need some things from town, Jake."

"What things?" Jake asked, gazing at the shelves of supplies cluttering the warehouse.

"Liniment for the horses. Jace Harrison's got it at his store. Mabel Harrison's got some piecework she's done for Miranda, and you can fetch that, too. Tell them I'll settle up when I come in on Friday."

"I don't suppose the liniment would wait till you got in yourself, huh? Nor the other things."

"Horses can go lame, Jake."

"I suppose."

"And did you ever know Miranda to wait on anything?" the colonel asked. "She's already badgered me for a week. Save me from the torture, won't you, Jake?"

"Be glad to, Colonel," Jake said, grinning. "You know, one of these days I'm going to find myself regular work, and you won't have to save up things for me to do."

"Jacob Henry, one of the joys a man gets from living as long as I have is that he can do what he wants with his money. If he decides to pay a few dollars to a scraggly-haired refugee from a mud wallow like you, it's his privilege to do so."

"I appreciate it all the same."

"You get that grateful grin off your face," Colonel Duncan demanded. "The day you don't do what's called for is the day you can think yourself taking something for nothing. You ever do that, Jake?"

"No, sir," Jake said, gazing seriously at the colonel's sober eyes. "Never will, either."

"Good. That's what I expect of you. Now hurry back and eat up that steak. If there's fritters, send one along to me. I'm particular fond of 'em."

"Yes, sir," Jake agreed.

"Miranda'll have your money for you when you get back. You know her. She won't let me touch the money box."

"Probably for the best," Jake said, grinning. "Elsewise you'd be as broke as Pa."

3

Jake found Miranda Duncan waiting impatiently in the dining room. Nearby, a platter of scrambled eggs sat beside a plate nearly filled by a pan-fried steak. There was a basket of round-shaped batter balls sprinkled with corn kernels, too. Fritters! He grinned away her frown and sat down at a waiting chair.

"The colonel said he could eat one of those fritters," Jake said as he cut himself a slice of steak.

"I ought to take him the whole basket," she grumbled. "The eggs will be cold before you get half through with them."

"Cold as ice they'll be a treat," he said between bites. "I believe a man could eat one of your breakfasts, Miranda, and go hungry for a week."

"Seems to me that's just what you do, Jake Wetherby," she complained. "I worry to think how skinny those brothers of yours have become. Betsy's far too pretty to be much of a cook."

"Oh?" Jake asked, laughing. "You're a fair hand with a skillet, and I don't see how it's uglied you any."

"Is that supposed to be a compliment?" she asked.

"Backhanded one, I'd say," Jerry Platt observed from the bar. "You got anything going to Dallas on the stage, Miss Miranda?"

"Nothing Nathaniel won't already have loaded," she barked. "You were leaving by and by, weren't you?"

"Got to keep to my schedule," the driver said, laughing. "I'll go round up the passengers. Miz Lassiter's maybe got herself scalped."

Jerry set off outside, and Miranda swept off to the warehouse with the bowl of fritters. She returned shortly with only half the fritters to find Jake hard at work devouring his steak.

"He told you of the piece goods, didn't he?" she asked as she sat across from him.

"I'll bring 'em along," Jake promised.

"I have a list of notions, too. Thread, some sewing needles, and other odds and ends."

"I'll take care of it," Jake added, accepting the list with his right hand and stuffing it into his shirt pocket. He then silently cleaned his plate and gobbled the fritters while Miranda sat, quietly watching.

"You could bring your brothers by some morning for a feed," she whispered when he set his napkin on the empty plate and sighed. "We never get all the eggs eaten."

"Not enough passengers stopping these days, huh?" Jake asked.

"Not enough willing to pay. Or able."

"Pa wouldn't abide the little boys coming," Jake noted. "I might rope Jericho into it, though. He's grown skinnier'n a matchstick, what with getting taller and all."

"Pa might manage some work for him, too."

"I wouldn't mind the company, even if Jer does have a temper."

"I've got one myself," Miranda confessed as she rose from the table. She took the egg platter, empty plate, and fritter bowl and headed for the kitchen. When she returned, Jake was standing by the door.

"Best I get along," he told her.

"Sure," she said, nodding. "You promise to have those things here before supper, don't you?"

"Yes'm," Jake assured her.

"Maybe you'll stay and eat with us. I'll have a fresh cobbler baked."

"I'd be a fool to pass that up," Jake said, taking her hand and giving it a light squeeze. "I'll fetch the things from the Harrisons and be back in no time."

"Send along my best to Mabel," Miranda urged. "And take special care with those piece goods. I don't want the lace mangled."

"Do my best, ma'am," Jake said, giving her a sham bow and then racing off before she could find anything to throw.

Jake nodded to Jerry Platt, who was herding his passengers into the stage, waved to Jefferson and Nathaniel, and then trotted over to where Maizy was drinking from the water trough.

"Time to go, girl," he whispered as he

untied the mare's reins. He then climbed atop, swung Maizy around toward Spring Creek, and began the short ride to Harrison's store.

Maizy wasn't the spriest horse in Texas, but she hated being tied. Once released from her temporary restraint, she bounded with unusual energy southeastward. Jake had a notion to splash across the creek and head cross-country, avoiding the farms that spread out on either side of Spring Creek.

"You'd like that, wouldn't you, girl?" he whispered to the mare. In spite of Maizy's lively gait, Jake decided against it. He headed instead toward the Chandler place.

He was still a quarter mile away when he spotted Christian Anders wading across the creek.

"That's not the way to school, Christy," Jake observed.

The ten-year-old glanced up in surprise. A rare mix of urgency and concern flooded his face. He swept a hank of yellow hair from his eyes and sighed.

"You saved me a hard walk, Jake," Christian explained. "Was on my way to Colonel Duncan's to find help. You'll do."

"What's happened?" Jake asked.

"Best pull me up behind you and ride on to the Chandler place. See for yourself."

Jake waited for the boy to step out of the creek and shake his legs dry. Then Christian climbed up onto Maizy's rump.

"What's got you all frazzled, Christy?" Jake asked. "I haven't seen you all lathered up and shivery since Si Garrett told you about that ghost that walks Rowlett Creek."

"Wish it was a ghost this time," the boy mumbled. "It's your papa, Jake."

"Pa?" Jake asked, growing cold.

"Had himself an accident," Christian explained. "Working on that fool dam. I don't know how it happened, but his leg got caught in the rocks. He near drowned."

"Go on," Jake said, feeling the youngster's hands clawing his back.

"Broke his left leg mighty bad. Pa and Sam Chandler got him pulled out onto dry land, but he's bad hurt and near froze."

"Somebody's gone for Doc Springfield, I suppose."

"Might be," Christian answered. "Amy's gone to your place."

"Won't be anybody there but Betsy and the baby," Jake grumbled. "The boys'll be headed for school."

"I'd be there myself if little Ben Chandler hadn't caught Amy and me on the way. We got Pa, and Amy went down to your place. I went—"

"I don't suppose Amy was on horseback, was she?" Jake broke in.

"Now you know she doesn't have a riding horse, and Pa won't have us riding the team."

"Then it's me that best get to town," Jake said, kicking Maizy into a gallop. He closed the quarter mile to the Chandlers' in no time, let Christian slide off the horse, and climbed down himself.

"Thank the Lord," Edna Chandler said,

glancing up from the creek bank. Beside her, wrapped in a heavy quilt, knelt her husband Sam. Little Ben sat on a nearby rock, gazing past Chris Anders at a pale and shivering Joe Wetherby.

Jake thought for a moment his father was dead. Joe Wetherby lay motionless, his two hundred fifty pounds shrunk and withered like a melon left too long on the vine. His eyes stared vacantly at the sky, and his breathing was so shallow his chest hardly moved.

"He's not—" Jake began.

"No, he's all right," Chandler answered as Jake took his father's hand. "Leg's pure shattered, though, and I fear we didn't help it much pulling him up here."

"It's no easy job hauling a man that big anywhere," Chris Anders observed.

"Pa, can you hear me?" Jake called. "Pa?"

"Jacob Henry?" Joe responded. "I'm cold, son. So cold."

"Can't you cover him some?" Jake asked.

"Ma, get some blankets," Chandler said, shaking himself out of a stupor.

"Jake, you best ride into town and fetch Doc Springfield," Edna said before turning toward the house. "It would be better to splint that leg before moving him."

"She's right," Anders agreed. "He may be lame already."

"I'm gone," Jake said, climbing back onto Maizy's back and urging the mare into a gallop. He then headed downstream toward what passed for the town of Harrison's Crossroads.

It wasn't far—certainly not more than five miles. Jake covered it in a little more than a quarter hour. He passed Amy Anders and Betsy along the way, but he didn't even pause. Betsy would find out for herself about Joe, and fetching the doctor was more important.

Once he got to the huddle of buildings that nestled on a slight rise above Spring Creek, Jake turned past Harrison's store and halted at the doctor's simple frame house. The doc was out front, digging in a small garden, and he sprang to his feet when he heard Maizy's approaching hooves.

"Trouble, Jake?" he asked.

"Pa's gone and broken a leg," Jake explained. "Up at the Chandler place."

"Know how to get a buggy hitched up?" Dr. Springfield asked.

"I imagine... I can... manage it," Jake replied as he fought to catch his breath.

"Tend it, then," the doctor urged. "Your pa won't be walking home. I'll go tell Jane Mary. She'll want to come along."

"Yes, sir," Jake said, dismounting.

The doctor and Jane Mary, Jake's sister, were on good terms, being neighbors. Her husband, Martin Browning, made and repaired tack when he wasn't keeping the town's post office, and Jane Mary usually found time to give the doc a hand with his four motherless young children.

"She's becoming a fair to middling nurse, too," Martin liked to boast. Jake thought she might have a chance to demonstrate that skill on their father.

By the time Jake had the doc's coal-black gelding harnessed to the buggy, Dr. Springfield had assembled a medical kit and brought Jane Mary over from next door.

"How bad is he?" Jane Mary asked as she climbed atop the leather bench that sat in the front of the small fourwheeled cart. Only Doc Springfield regarded it as a buggy. To anyone else it was a short-bed wagon.

"The leg didn't took so bad," Jake explained, "but he was whiter'n a sheet. Near frozen, I'd guess."

"Working in a creek this time of year," the doctor grumbled as he whipped the gelding into motion. "It's a miracle half the county's not dead of exposure!"

The doctor went on to profess the merits of indoor bathing in heated tubs as a cure for most maladies, but Jake wasn't listening. He pulled out Miranda's list and raced over to Harrison's store. A promise, after all, was a promise!

Actually, it didn't take but a few minutes for Mabel Harrison to assemble the piece goods and supplies in a box. Jake took the bundle without comment and tied it behind his saddle. He caught up with the doctor just shy of Franklin Selwyn's farm, and the three of them rode together the rest of the way.

"I don't suppose you could forget about the colonel just once and worry over Pa," Jane Mary grumbled as they passed the family farm.

"What good would it do Pa?" Jake asked. "I've got my obligations, and with Pa abed with a broken leg, we're apt to need any money I can bring in."

"He's right about that, Jane Mary," Doc agreed. "And he caught us easily enough."

"Maybe," she admitted. Jake scowled. He knew she was worried, and Jane Mary always expected her brothers to follow her lead. She'd never understand you could worry without falling to pieces.

When they finally arrived at the Chandler place, Jake found little had changed. Edna had piled some blankets onto Joe Wetherby, but no one had thought to kindle a fire or strip the freezing man's soggy clothing from him.

"Fools," the doctor muttered when he climbed off the buggy. "Jane Mary, let's get this leg set quick. Be a miracle if he's not caught his death already!"

Jake dismounted and helped his sister cut away their father's trousers. They then pulled on the heel while Dr. Springfield adjusted the fractured bones into their proper positions. Afterward the splinting went rapidly.

Joe Wetherby never even whimpered all the while. Jake felt the icy touch of his father's skin and knew it wasn't Joe Wetherby's tolerance for pain that muted a cry. No, big as he was, Joe was prone to wailing and cursing when discomfort was at hand. Only after Jane Mary got water heated, and she and Betsy bathed the flesh and rubbed it dry, did some color return to Joe Wetherby's bearded face.

"Hurts, darling," he whispered.

"Rest easy, Joe," Betsy answered. "We'll have you along home before long."

In truth, though, they were better than an

hour getting the washing done, and even with everyone working together, it was past noon before they worked Joe Wetherby's burly body off the creek bank and into the buggy's bed.

"We'll need help getting him into the house, too," Jane Mary told the others.

"I'll come along," Sam Chandler volunteered.

"We're headed south anyway," Chris Anders added.

"I appreciate it," Jake said, speaking for his father. "All you've done."

"Neighbors do for each other," Anders insisted.

"When your pa's well, we'll have a real celebration," Edna Chandler added as she hugged her little son to her side.

"Barn dance maybe," Anders suggested. "I know a gal who wouldn't object to that."

Amy blushed, and Jake grinned at the notion of her stomping around a square with little Jericho.

"Coming, Jake?" Jane Mary called from the buggy.

"Sure," Jake said, mounting Maizy and nudging the mare into a trot.

It was late afternoon when Jake delivered the Harrisons' parcel to Miranda Duncan. She met him at the door with a surprised expression.

"I wasn't expecting you so early," she said as she took the package. "Supper's not ready."

"I can't stay anyway," he told her.

"Why not?" she asked. When he didn't explain immediately, she gripped his hand and led the way inside the dining room. "What's happened?" she whispered.

"Pa broke a leg," Jake explained.

"He's not the first to do it," she noted. "Nor will he be the last. I guess Doc Springfield's had a look at it."

"Sure," Jake replied. "It's not the leg that troubles me, though. Those fools left him lying there, shivering with cold. Doc says he could turn worse."

"How much worse?"

"Whole lot worse," Jake said, shuddering. "That sort of chill can bring on lung fever. It's what killed Ma."

"Hot broths can fight that off," Miranda said as she set the box on the bar and fished out a money box. She took out three silver dollars and passed them into Jake's hand. "I'll bring a food basket down first chance."

"Thanks," Jake said, pocketing the money. "Miz Anders brought something along, and you know the Selwyns. They'll be happening along with enough to feed an army for a month. We've got plenty already, and Betsy can cook."

"Can she?" Miranda asked. "With a sick husband and a baby to mind?"

"Jane Mary will stay and do the nursing," Jake explained. "There's no keeping her away. The boys and I'll see to the rest."

"It's no crime, accepting help, Jake."

"Not if it's needed," he agreed. "May come a time, Miranda. Just now we're fine."

"You'll let me know?" she asked.

"Be busy for a time, but we'll see each other again."

"When?" she asked, gripping his hands with ironlike fingers.

"By and by," he assured her. "By and by."

4

When Jake returned home that afternoon, he discovered a small army of visitors camped on his father's porch. Neighbors had brought food, and well-wishers stood by with prayers and tonics to hurry Joe back to health. Betsy greeted each in turn and accepted their gifts good-naturedly.

"I can abide most of them," Jane Mary pronounced as she sniffed at a particularly noxious mason jar. "These homemade remedies are mostly alcohol and part poison, though. You'd think grown people would know better."

"They mean well," Betsy insisted.

"Good intentions will get you just as dead," Jane Mary grumbled as she poured the tonic out the window. "Maybe it'll kill weeds."

Jake left the women to oversee his father's health. He didn't know a thing about doctoring, and when he did glance in, he saw a Joe Wetherby who was fast asleep.

"The best thing you can do for him," Doe Springfield told Jake, "is look after your brothers and bend a knee. Prayer can work miracles, you know."

"Yes, sir," Jake agreed. Praying hadn't helped his mother, though. Jane Mary and the doctor, who were certain to know best, had concern etched deeply across their brows.

Things got no better when the boys returned from school that afternoon. They'd gotten the news of Joe's accident at the Selwyn place, and all three boys appeared at the house breathless from a hard run.

"Where's Pa?" Jericho huffed.

"He's not dead, is he?" Jordy demanded.

Josh, who was white with exertion, dropped to his knees and tried to find words. Jake threw the eleven-year-old across one shoulder and led the way inside.

Jane Mary guarded their father's door like a sentry, but reading her brothers' fearful faces, she opened the door and let them pass. Joe Wetherby lay as before, pale and still, with a comforter tucked up next to his chin.

"Pa?" Jordy asked, touching Joe's exposed left hand. "He's cold, Jake."

"Lay in the creek for a time," Jake explained. "He'll be a while getting his color back, but there's no hurry. He can't move around on a busted leg anyhow."

"He going to get better, Jane Mary?" Josh asked, huddling beside her. "Huh?"

"Should be just fine," she answered. "Don't you worry yourself over Pa. He's a bear, remember? What's a little cold to a man like him?"

"He doesn't look like a bear," Jericho observed. "Once Ma took to her bed, she never got up again."

"Fool dam," Jordy muttered. "Everyone knew it was a stupid idea to begin with. Now Pa's got himself froze building it. What for? Nothing!"

"Shhhh," Jane Mary scolded. "Hush. You boys have chores waiting, and lessons besides, I'd wager. Get along after them. Later Pa may wake, and you'll want time to visit him then."

"Sure," Jericho said, waving his younger brothers along. "Work's waiting."

Jake watched the three boys leave. He then studied Jane Mary's face.

"Can't be too bad," he whispered. "Doc went back to town."

"Nothing he could do," she explained. "Let Pa rest. See he eats and rests."

"He will get better, won't he?" Jake asked.

"Has to," Jane Mary mumbled. "They need him."

The words lacked conviction, and Jake glanced back at their father. What if Joe Wetherby died? It would make no difference to Jane Mary, her being married and all. The farm would pass down to Betsy, he supposed. He could fend for himself, but what about the boys?

"Cross that bridge when you come to it, Jake," Jane Mary advised, as if reading his thoughts. "With some sleep and broth, Pa will come around directly."

"Sure," Jake replied. He then stepped past her and walked on outside. Jericho was chopping stove wood, and the sounds of the heavy ax splintering hackberry logs resounded across the land. Jordy and Josh were occupied looking after the animals. If not for the image of his father's pale face, Jake would have judged everything perfectly normal. Except, perhaps, that it was too quiet.

Those next few days, subtle changes came to the farm. The boys grew more and more quarrelsome. Betsy tried without success to restore peace and then retreated to an old maple rocker with the baby.

"We have to pull together," Jane Mary argued. Her constant vigil had painted dark circles under her eyes, though, and she was as cross as anyone. Worse, Joe opened his eyes only at mealtime, and he never spoke.

"He's shrinking away, Jake," Jericho noted. "Just like Ma did."

"There's an awful lot of Pa to shrink," Jake argued. "Don't go burying him just yet."

That Sunday, Jake hitched the mules to the old wagon that had brought the family west from Tennessee.

"The circuit preacher's coming to Rowlett Creek," he announced. "I suspect if we go to the meeting they're having there, our prayers might get on up to heaven a hair faster."

"I've got no shoes that fit," Jordy grumbled. "Ma couldn't abide going to meeting barefoot."

"God wouldn't notice," Josh insisted. "Jake's right. We ought to go."

"You can wear mine, Jordy," Jericho suggested. "Stuff some rags in the toes and they'll fit."

"And what do you plan to wear?" Jake asked.

"I haven't got a fit shirt, Jake," Jericho explained.

"I'd judge that white one of mine would do," Jake said, studying Jericho's eyes. "I can wear the blue one."

"Then I'm without shoes again," Jordy complained.

"I can wear my boots," Jake said. "You take Jer's, and he can wear my store-bought ones. Now, is everything settled?"

"Just about," Jericho said, frowning. "Got some time, Jake? I got something personal to ask."

"Yeah?" Jordan asked with a grin.

"You get yourself and Josh ready," Jake instructed. "Jer, let's get some water from the well."

The two older brothers then stepped outside. Halfway to the well Jericho explained.

"It's chin whiskers," he said, scratching his chin. "Boys years younger have started cutting theirs off, and the boys at school are calling me Billy Goat Wetherby on account of mine."

"You've got a razor," Jake noted. "Cut 'em off."

"How?" Jericho asked. "I figured Pa would show me, but he's been busy. And now—"

"Wouldn't hurt me to shave, either," Jake said, grinning "I guess I can give you a lesson."

"I don't want to cut myself," Jericho insisted as he lowered a bucket down the shaft.

"Wouldn't want anybody thinking I got in a fight or something."

"Anybody?" Jake asked. "Or Amy?"

Jericho hid his face, and Jake laughed.

"I believe we can turn you into a respectable churchgoer, little brother," Jake vowed. "Anything else you'll have to manage on your own, though."

"Wouldn't want it elsewise," Jericho said, blushing.

And so Jake Wetherby undertook his eldest brother's tonsorial education. It went fairly well. Jericho only nicked himself once, and it was barely worth mentioning. A splash of cold water slowed the bleeding, and there was hardly a scab by the time they climbed into the wagon and set off for Rowlett Creek.

"Aren't you coming?" Jake asked Betsy.

"My place's here," she answered. Her eyes were red and moist. She appeared lost.

"I'll mind the baby," Jane Mary offered.

"You've got enough to look after," Betsy replied. "Baby Joe's mine to watch."

Jake gazed at the two women. There had never really been much affection between them, but just then an uneasy truce seemed to have settled around the house. Jake nodded and poked the mules into motion. Soon they were splashing across Spring Creek and heading along north to the clapboard meetinghouse where the traveling Methodist preacher spoke once a month to the people of southern Collin County.

Jake had hoped to get there early and settle in before the preacher arrived, but the circuit rider was an early riser, and he had assembled the younger children in the meetinghouse so he could share some message or other. That left the Wetherby boys to linger outside close to half an hour. They were besieged with questions about their father's condition, and Jake thought he might drown in the sea of pity that followed.

"How's Jane Mary holding up?" Martin asked.

"She's worn out," Jake told his brother-in-law. "We all try to spell her, but there's no arguing with her."

"She's headstrong, and that's a truth," Martin admitted. "I thought I might hire a woman to come out and help."

"It wouldn't make much difference, I expect," Jake argued. "And we don't have the money."

"Even if Pa Wetherby rights himself, this winter'll be hard," Martin noted. "I've been thinking how maybe I could take Jordy or Josh in and teach them the saddlery trade."

"Ma wanted them to finish their schooling first," Jake said, sighing, "Of course, Jane Mary could see to the lessons."

"Yeah, she sees to most everything," Martin agreed. "And everybody."

Jake grinned a reply. Then the preacher called everyone inside. The little ones scampered out to enjoy their freedom, carrying Josh along with them. Jake turned to fetch his brother, but Martin halted him.

"Let the boy run some," Martin suggested. "He's had few chances lately, I suspect."

There was truth in those words.

"He's right," Jordy said, nodding, and Jake let things lie. He was glad once the preacher began, too, for the sermonizing was deep and profound.

As a general rule, Jake didn't much care for indoor preaching. He'd always found God riding the wind or sitting in the clouds after a summer rain. Bright stars and yellow flowers promised more eternity than the best honey-mouthed man ever born.

Reverend Darnell Middleton spoke with an old man's anger and a young man's zeal. He quoted scripture and promised damnation to the wicked. By the time he was halfway, though, a good portion of the children were sweating and most of the men were counting toes. It wasn't what Jake wanted or needed, and he was sorry for coming. Worse, Reverend Middleton spoke far too long and sorrowfully about the untimely death of little Harvey Lindale.

"Don't grieve for him, though, brothers and sisters," the preacher declared, "He's gone to his glory, to that land where the streets are paved with gold and the angels sing in perfect harmony."

Afterward, as the people spilled outside, Jericho moaned aloud.

"Streets of gold?" Jordy whispered. "Sounds like a cold place to me, and Pa can't abide singing. Wish he'd heard. Likely he'd be sure to get himself well."

"Or head to the other place," Jericho suggested.

41

"No, he'll want to be with Ma," Jake insisted. His brothers lost their grins, and Jake was instantly sorry he'd spoken. Jordy raced over and grabbed Josh.

"You'd be welcome at our house for supper, boys," Rebecca Selwyn offered as she rounded up her own litter of youngsters.

"I appreciate it, ma'am," Jake answered. "Truth is, we'll never get half the food eaten that's been brought by. We're not wanting for anything."

"Except for Pa to get well," Josh was quick to add.

"That most of all," Jericho agreed.

"Well, our prayers are with him," Mrs. Selwyn said, bending over and giving Josh a quick kiss on the forehead. Jordy and Jericho were quick to skip away, but she managed to collar Jake and give him a peck.

"Thanks for the concern, ma'am," Jake told her as he fought to chase the redness from his face.

"Jane Mary's out there, you know," Martin added, stepping between the boys and a crowd of well-wishers. "Matter of fact, she's sure to be waiting dinner on us already."

"We better hurry, then," Jake said, taking the hint and urging his brothers toward the wagon. No sooner were they piled in the bed than Jake whipped the mules into motion. Martin rode alongside, whistling a spry tune.

"It's not that I mind meetings exactly," Martin said afterward. "I rather take to the singing. It's just that all the sermonizing puts my backside to sleep, stiffens up my neck, and puts me in a sour disposition for a month. Lucky we don't have a regular preacher, I guess."

"Guess so," Jordy agreed, laughing.

"Can't blame meeting for that, though," Jericho objected. "I remember Reverend Goddard. He was always smiling, and he never had anything sour to say. It's this young fellow with all his talk of burning sulfur and eternal punishment. Can't scare a fellow into behaving. Got to make him want to do good."

"He scared me plenty," Jordy insisted. "And by the look of Mr. Harrison and Allie Halle, I'd say there were some others feeling the heat of those burning rocks, too."

"Fire and brimstone's an old remedy for frontier sin," Martin observed, "But I'm with Jer. Give me ten Pop Goddards for every young fountain of wildfire like Darnell."

Jake halfway smiled to hear them picking apart that meeting. Then Martin told about a South Texas baptism he remembered from his growing-up days. It seemed some pious old grandmother lost her false teeth in the river, and the brethren spent half a day looking for them.

"And that wasn't the worst of it," Martin went on to say. "Young Ben Lively, who lived up to his name most times, went for a swim afterward, and the whole congregation happened across him sitting stark naked on the riverbank. He thought everybody'd gone home, you see, but he couldn't know about Miz Fleetwood's teeth!"

The brothers broke out laughing as they imagined that surprised boy, and they didn't stop till Jake drove the mules through the shallows of Spring Creek and up the far bank toward home.

"I'm grateful you came along, Marty," Jake said afterward as he freed the mules from their harness. "We were all in need of a laugh. Especially the little ones."

"Was a good notion all around," Martin explained. "I was in need of company. And somebody else's cooking."

"Bet we've got some peach pie," Jake suggested. "And who knows what the women have cooked up for supper!"

"You know, Jake, it's strange now you mention it, but I can't sniff anything on the wind," Martin observed. "No cooking at all."

Jake took a deep breath and nodded sadly. He left the mules and raced into the house.

"Better head into town," Jane Mary said when Jake stumbled through the door of his father's room. Jordy and Josh stood on either side of Jericho, on the far side of the bed. Betsy nursed Baby Joe in the rocker. Joe Wetherby sat propped up on two feather pillows. His face was pale as death, and he held a bloody kerchief to his lips.

"He's coughing blood, Jake," a worried Jericho said.

"Like Ma," Jake muttered.

"Tell Doc," Jane Mary urged. "Ask him to stop by and have a look."

"Isn't much he can do," Jake said, stepping over and gripping his father's bearlike hand. "Pa?"

"Fetch him, son," Joe said faintly. He then coughed violently, sending shivers up Jake's back. "Take your brothers along outside, too."

"Come on, boys," Jake said, releasing his father's hand and pointing to the door. "I have to ride to town. You'll have to tend the mules."

Jericho led Jordy and Josh outside, and Jake nodded to his father.

"I guess he's dying, huh?" Jake whispered as he passed his sister.

Jane Mary answered with a grim nod.

5

Jake arrived in town half an hour later, but he found Doc Springfield busy.

"It's Mrs. Halle," Mabel Harrison explained. "She's having her baby."

Jake left word of his father's worsening condition and returned home. When the doctor finally arrived around dusk, he spent only a few minutes with Joe Wetherby.

"What'd he say?" Jake asked Jane Mary afterward, when she stepped outside a moment.

"He left some drops I can give to help ease the pain, but it's up to Pa to shake off the fever," she said. "Even if he does, I don't think it will much matter. He's coughing up his lungs, just like Ma."

"He won't last till Christmas," Jake mumbled.

Betsy appeared in the doorway. "Your pa wants to talk to the two of you," she explained, waving them inside.

Jake hesitated, but Jane Mary pulled him along inside. They stood together on one side of the bed while Betsy sat on the opposite corner, holding Baby Joe.

"You're feeling better," Jane Mary said, forcing a smile onto her face.

"The drops," Joe said, nodding. "Helps with the pain."

"Leg bothering you, Pa?" Jake asked.

"No, not so much," Joe replied. "It's my chest. Not so different than with Mary Elizabeth."

"You're strong, Pa," Jane Mary said, rubbing a tear from her eye. "You'll fight off the fever and be yourself again in no time."

"You know better, daughter," Joe told her. "We talked that much through before Doc Springfield got here. Time's short, I figure. Might be it's for the best."

"Pa?" Jake asked.

"I wouldn't do any of you much good lying here in bed."

"You'd be up again soon," Jane Mary argued.

"No," Betsy said, frowning. "He wouldn't."

"How do you know?" Jake asked.

"Because I told her," Joe explained. "Jacob Henry, now your sister's taken a husband, you're eldest. It's up to you to look after the others. There's a hard time coming, and you'll need to be strong."

"I know," Jake said, biting his lip. "It's sure to be harder on the others."

"Maybe not harder," Joe said, coughing. "But

46

you're better able to fend for yourself. I look at Joshua and Jordan, and they seem so small."

"They're Wetherbys, though," Jake declared. "They'll get past the hurt."

"Sure," Jane Mary agreed. Her legs wobbled a bit then, and Jake caught her an instant before she fell.

"Daughter, you're dead on your feet," Joe scolded. "You have to get some rest."

"Later," Jane Mary argued.

"Now," her father insisted.

"Marty should take you home," Jake advised.

"No, I'll be fine," she argued. "Just let me rest a bit."

"I'll mind Pa," Jake offered.

"That's for me to do," Betsy said, gazing up at them. "I haven't been much help up to now, but I will be."

"The baby—" Jane Mary began.

"Isn't much trouble," Betsy said, smiling. "He's a comfort, to be honest. Go on home, Jane Mary. You have a husband to look after. So do I."

"We'll be here," Jake added, gripping his sister's hands.

"That's another thing," Betsy said, turning toward Joe.

"You boys have let your chores go," Joe noted.

"Starting tomorrow you'll manage them better, won't you?" Betsy asked.

"Sure," Jake said, studying his stepmother's face. It seemed as if a girl was miraculously changing into a woman before his eyes.

"I know you don't think much of me," Betsy told them, "and lately there's been good reason. I mean to do right by Joe, though. We may not have a lot of time left, but we'll make it count for something."

"Pa?" Jane Mary asked.

"It's how I want it," Joe insisted.

"Then I guess it's time I went home," Jane Mary said, frowning.

"Jane Mary?" Jake cried in surprise.

"As for you, Jacob Henry, grab those brothers and ride out to the wood lot," Joe suggested. "Camp there a day or so. Leave your ma and me to sort all this out.

"We've got chores," Jake argued.

"They'll wait till Tuesday," Betsy argued. "Won't hurt the boys to miss school one day. Shoot us a deer, Jake. Fresh venison would be welcome."

"Do the youngsters good to forget about... things," Jake's father told him. "Get away from this place, son. Death's hanging in the air so thick I can taste it."

"I want to be here when... when you..." Jake stammered.

"I'm not going anywhere tomorrow," Joe grumbled. "Later on I'll have some things to talk over with you."

"We haven't spoken a dozen words since—" Jake began.

"I know," Joe cut him off. "Collect the boys, Jacob Henry. Leave tonight. Shoot your deer and swap some of those tall tales Silas Garrett's so fond of telling. Try to forget."

"You figure it's possible?" Jake asked.

"Not altogether," Joe admitted. "But you'll find the distraction welcome, I suspect."

"And if you won't, the others will," Betsy added.

"We'll be home in time to tend the animals Tuesday morning," Jake promised.

"I'll expect you," Betsy replied. "Have bacon and eggs ready for all four of you."

"Fair enough," Jake said, swallowing hard.

"I'd appreciate it if you managed a kind word for your ma by and by," Joe added. "She's going to need a strong arm to lean on."

Jake scowled. He couldn't manage to promise anything, but he vowed to try to remain on good terms with Betsy for his father's sake.

"Well, get along now," Joe urged.

Jane Mary raced out the door. Jake followed more slowly.

"We're going on back to town," Jane Mary announced when Jake joined her and Martin on the porch.

"Maybe he's right and it's best," Jake replied.

"I don't suppose when all's said and done it much matters," Jane Mary muttered.

"No, I expect not," Jake agreed.

Half an hour later Jake led his three brothers north toward the thirty-acre wood lot his father had bought along Rowlett Creek. Soon they would take the wagon up there and begin cutting oak and willow logs for winter fuel. That evening they walked. Jake carried a long-barreled Kentucky rifle. Jericho followed with a provision bag filled with salt pork, corn bread, and the remains of a peach pie. Josh carried blankets and candles, while Jordy held a torch high to light the way.

"I never much liked this place," Jordy grumbled as they entered the shadowy wood.

"There's haunts hereabouts," Josh added. "Jer's seen 'em."

"Not for a time now," Jericho noted. "Mostly downstream then."

"Could be bears around, though," Jordy suggested. "Wolves!"

"Or Comanches," Josh said, shuddering. "Maybe we should head on back home."

"There's nothing out here we haven't seen before," Jake assured them. "We've seen plenty of wolves, haven't we, Jer? Remember those two that tried to raid our chickens last winter?"

"Coyotes," Jericho grumbled. "Not real wolves. Coons are a fair sight more bother. We fought one or two of them before."

"Like that one that raided our camp on the way from Tennessee!" Jordy exclaimed. "Bigger'n Josh by twenty pounds, I'll bet."

"He was big, all right," Jake agreed, "but this rifle of mine made short work of him."

"That rifle and Sandy," Jericho noted. "Wish I still had that dog. Sandy was a real prize."

"First Sandy," Josh said, sighing, "then Ma. Now—"

"Don't you say it!" Jordy shouted. "Nothing's going to happen to Pa."

At least not tonight, Jake thought as he waved Jordy onto a narrow trail.

They made camp near a small spring and built up a fire. In the distance an owl hooted in alarm. The sound echoed down the creek, giving the place an eerie feel.

"Build up the fire," Jordy urged.

Jericho rolled a couple of big oak logs onto the flames and rolled his blanket out between Jordy and Josh. When Jake located his bed on the opposite side of the fire, all three brothers moved over beside him.

"Not worried about an owl, are you?" Jake asked.

"Remember what Si said the Indians believe?" Jericho asked. "Owl's a bad omen. Means somebody's going to die."

"So what are we supposed to do?" Jake asked, laughing. "Sprinkle salt on our noses or circle a horseshoe three times?"

Josh and Jordy laughed. Si Garrett was famous for his superstitions and the crazy rituals he would perform to counter evil omens.

"Settle yourselves down and get some rest," Jericho urged. "We'll scare up a deer tomorrow if we're up early enough."

"Or if something doesn't scare us up tonight," Josh said, kicking off his boots. "Keep that rifle handy, Jake."

"It's loaded, but I've got the cap safe in my pocket," Jake explained. "So if a bear eats me, grab a spare cap from my cartridge belt."

"Sure," Jericho said, laughing. Jordy and Josh found the notion less humorous. Scurrying squirrels and prowling raccoons managed

51

to keep the younger boys up most of that night.

Jake slept a bit more. His brothers' thrashing around woke him twice, but he finally managed to settle Josh down by letting him nestle in alongside.

Pa was right, Jake told himself. They're pitiful small.

He dreamed that night of digging a grave on that lonely hill where their mother lay. Of planting flowers for them that next spring. Of telling Baby Joe of the father he couldn't remember.

When Jake finally cracked his eyes open, he discovered Jericho busy heating the corn bread and roasting pork strips on sticks.

"Venison will be an improvement," Jericho said, grinning at Jake's weary gaze. "I spied some tracks upriver. Fairsized ones. Likely we'll find a big buck. You figure you can make me some buttons out of the antlers like Frank Selwyn did for Si?"

"Easy enough to do if you've got the antlers," Jake answered. "It's the season for it."

"I could do with a buckskin jacket," Jordy said, pulling his blanket around his shoulders to fend off the crisp morning chill. "Be like Daniel Boone."

"Davy Crockett," Jericho argued. "You're in Texas now."

"Before you go figuring what to do with the skin and antlers, maybe we should shoot this buck," Jake grumbled.

"That's your job," Jordy said. "You got the rifle."

"I ought to have my own gun, don't you think, Jake?" Jericho asked. "Jordy, too. We're not little boys anymore."

"That's for Pa to decide," Jake answered.

His brothers gazed at him sadly. Pretty soon it would be Jake who would decide. They all knew it. The thought shook Jake right down to the bone.

They gobbled up squares of corn bread and chewed pork strips. Then, after rolling up the blankets and stashing them in the crook of a big live oak, Jake led the way upstream to where Jericho said he spotted deer tracks. They found them easily enough, and a half mile farther on they saw the deer themselves.

Jake counted seven, five does and two bucks. The best of the bucks had a rack of horns the equal of any Jake had ever seen. A second, smaller buck was closer. Jake aimed at that one.

Culling the herd, Colonel Duncan would have called it. Leave the strong to improve the herd. Pick off a lesser buck and leave the does to replenish the thickets.

One, two, three, Jake counted silently as he set the hammer at full cock, released a deep breath, and fired. The rifle emitted a sharp thwack, and powder smoke stung Jake's eyes. The deer instantly took flight—all save the second buck. It turned to its left and fell, struck just below the left shoulder by a ball that tore through heart and lungs.

"You got him!" Jordy shouted.

"Shot him dead!" Jericho cried.

"Now comes the work," Jake observed as he passed his rifle over to Jordy and marched toward the fallen deer. He dragged the carcass over to a nearby willow, tied its hind feet to a low branch, and cut the throat so the blood would drain. Later he skinned the animal and began the butchering.

It wasn't his favorite task, butchering. Jake always found himself growing faint at the sight and smell of blood. It was the same whenever Joe Wetherby determined it was time to kill a hog. Jericho always managed the work better. Sure, Jer might be a scamp, but he understood farm work. Jake, well, he considered himself a misfit.

"A farmer learns the land, son," Joe Wetherby must have told his son a thousand times.

"I'll never make even half a farmer, Pa," Jake had answered. "I may be picking corn, but my mind's off riding the hills beyond the creek, adventuring."

"Dreaming," his father had grumbled.

Jake imagined Joe Wetherby saw too much of himself in his eldest son. Where had dreams gotten Joe? Dead this time.

"Jake, you think maybe we can follow those deer and shoot another one?" Jordy asked. "That way Josh could have a coat, too."

"No, one's enough," Jake told them. "There's enough venison to feed us a good while. You don't kill animals just for their hides."

"Anyway, winter's a way off," Jericho observed. "We'll hunt again."

"Maybe one of these times you'll let me shoot," Jordy said.

"I think you should all have a try at it," Jake replied. "I believe next time I visit Colonel Duncan, I'll ask about buying one of those new rifles he's brought out from the East. He might have some older guns cheap, too."

"Pa won't spend the money," Jericho muttered.

"I've got some saved," Jake explained. "Could be the colonel would pay for a deer carcass or two to feed the stage passengers. He's bought catfish off me before."

"Plenty of times," Jordy agreed. "I'd dearly love to have a rifle of my own."

"Might be necessary, too," Jericho observed, "if Pa—"

Jake flashed an angry look, and Jericho swallowed the thought. For a brief while they were escaping death's shadow. No one wanted to hurry its return.

6

The brothers returned in time for Tuesday morning chores, as Jake had promised.

"I see you got your deer," Betsy observed. "Fresh venison has always been a welcome change from pork and chicken."

"Pa any better?" Jake asked.

"Some," she told him. "You boys seem some better yourselves."

It was the truth. For a short time they'd put the sadness behind them. Once the butchering was finished, there had been time for considerable pranking. Ghost stories and rowdy singing had chased the worst of their gloom away.

Those next few days Joe Wetherby seemed to brighten, too. He continued to cough, but his face regained a degree of color, and he got some solid food down.

"Might be you'll go and prove that doc wrong, Pa," Jake declared when his father managed to crutch his way into the kitchen.

"Wouldn't be surprised," Joe replied. "We Wetherbys are a hard batch to keep down."

Such hopes were premature, though. When a Blue Norther swept down on them the first week of November, Joe returned to his bed. The coughing grew worse, and Betsy began trying every snake oil tonic and backwoods remedy the neighbors brought by. Nothing helped. Joe wasted away before his family's eyes.

"I hoped maybe he'd hang on till Christmas, Jake," Jane Mary confided during one of her visits. "I don't imagine it's possible now."

"He hurts all the time," Jake said, sighing. "I stopped praying he'd get well. Hurts him too much. Now I just hope he'll find some rest."

"He will," Jane Mary assured Jake. "He'll be at peace soon."

Their father, too, sensed the end was drawing near. One by one he invited the boys to sit with him. Josh and Jordy left with eyes rubbed red and raw. Jericho managed to hold in the tears, but Jake heard him crying later, alone in their room.

Jake himself took the last turn. He'd begun spelling Betsy every second night anyway, and he was more accustomed to his father's shortened breath and occasional coughing spasms.

"You look worn down, Jacob Henry," Joe observed when Jake sat in the rocker beside the bed.

"No, I'm holding up," Jake replied.

"We'll all of us catch up on our rest soon, son," Joe declared. "Just now I've got a few things to say."

"Yes, sir?"

"I know we've had our share of quarrels, but I take no small share of pride in how you've stood tall since I broke my leg."

"Just doing my share, Pa," Jake said, taking a deep breath. "No different than anybody else."

"I know you didn't think too much of the mill idea. Guess you were right about that. I just hoped to manage something better for you boys. For Betsy. For the baby."

"I know, Pa."

"Your ma and I hoped Texas would be a fresh beginning for us all. Instead it's put an end to us."

"We've done all right," Jake argued.

"We've barely scratched out a living," Joe grumbled. "I know that, and you've seen it all along. What you might not know is I borrowed money against the place."

"Everybody does," Jake said, gripping his father's hand. "Don't worry yourself about it. We'll pay it off when we get next year's crop in."

57

Joe started to elaborate, but Jake hushed him.

"Pa, I'd judge you did all right by us. We may be Fitch runts, but there's Wetherby backbone there, too. We may have a fight ahead of us, but I figure we're up to it."

"Jake—"

"Pa, don't go worrying over us."

"I have to," Joe insisted, coughing violently. For a moment he couldn't stop, and again the kerchief reddened.

"Easy, Pa," Jake urged as he tried to alleviate his father's suffering.

"I have to... think of Betsy... and the baby," Joe said as he gasped for breath. "I know you... never thought much... of her as a... ma, but ..."

"She's grown some these past weeks," Jake said, sighing. "Can't expect me, or Jane Mary, either, to feel too comfortable with a gal not much older than ourselves taking charge."

"She's too gentle to weather the storm that's coming."

"I'll be here, Pa," Jake pledged. "Don't worry about that."

"I do," Joe insisted. "Can't help it. The farm—"

"Pa, don't you see? We've plowed. We've tended the orchard. There isn't a thing we haven't done before. Jer and I're near grown, and even Josh can work a corn row. We've got Marty and Jane Mary handy, and plenty of good friends besides."

"You don't know—"

"What I don't know, I'll learn," Jake vowed. "You can rely on me, Pa. Trust me to see to things."

Joe gazed deeply into Jake's eyes and smiled.

The big man nodded and lay his head back. His eyes closed and he fell into a light sleep.

"We'll talk more when you're better," Jake said, slipping his hand from his father's weary fingers.

As it turned out, though, Jake never spoke with his father after that night. The following evening, while Betsy kept watch, Joe Wetherby's chest rose and fell for the last time. When the boys rose to begin their morning chores, Betsy stood on the porch, waiting to pass on the grim news.

"Can't be," Jericho cried. "I was talking to him just yesterday!"

"Pa?" Jordy called.

Josh stepped over and fell against Jake's side.

"There are things to do," Betsy said, mustering her strength. "Jake, you should ride to town and tell Jane Mary. Have Jace Harrison send word to Dallas, asking that circuit preacher to come speak some words at the burying."

"Not him," Jake objected. "I'll ride over to the colonel's place and send a letter along to Pastor Goddard. That new fellow didn't even know Pa, and I don't want any hell and damnation preaching!"

"He's right," Jericho agreed. "Jake, you go see Colonel Duncan. I'll walk into town and tell Jane Mary."

"We should see about a proper box, too," Betsy said, scratching her head with one hand and easing Baby Joe onto the floor with the other. "A marker."

"I'll carve a board like the one we made for Ma," Jordy volunteered.

"We can make the coffin, too," Jake said. "Pa favored cedar wood. We've got some cedars up in the wood straight enough for good boards, and I can talk Mr. Selwyn out of some proper carpenter's tools."

"Then I suppose all that's left is to choose the churchyard," Betsy said, wiping a tear from her cheek.

"He should be up on the hill with Ma," Josh said, gazing up at his stepmother.

"It's what we'd like," Jake said, pulling his little brother closer. "If it doesn't trouble you too much."

"No, he should have company," she agreed. "Somebody he knows."

"I'll make the hole good and deep," Jake promised. "We can put up one of those little fences around it."

"Your father couldn't abide fences," Betsy argued. "No, it's best to mark the place with stones, I think."

"He'd like that," Jericho said, nodding. "We can whitewash 'em. Come spring plant flowers there."

"Yes, that's a fine notion," Betsy agreed.

And so they set out on their assigned tasks. By early afternoon neighbors and friends from town began stopping by with words of comfort and baskets of food. Jane Mary and Martin came to help with the arrangements. Si Garret brought his brother-in-law Frank Selwyn's toolbox out and helped Jake craft a coffin. It was no small task, considering Joe Wetherby's length and girth.

By the time Noah Goddard arrived two

days later, every preparation was complete. Joe's four sons, Martin Browning, and four neighbors carried the heavy coffin from the Wetherby wagon and lowered it silently into its waiting grave.

"I'm the resurrection," Pastor Goddard said solemnly. "I'm the light. Those are the Lord's words, and we can take comfort in them."

The gathering sang two hymns, even though Jordy insisted his father hated both of them, and Jake began shoveling dirt over the box.

"Rest easy, Pa," he whispered. "I'll mind things here."

The wind seemed to whisper an answer, and Jake nodded soberly.

Texas grew cold that next week. A light snow dusted the land, and it seemed to Jake the whole country was frozen, dead.

"Listen to the wind," Jericho urged. "It's moaning!"

Dark clouds swallowed the stars and smothered the sun. Even when the snow melted away, a numbing cold lingered.

"What do we do now Pa's gone?" Jordy asked.

"Go on doing our chores," Jake explained. "Patch the roof when it needs it. Feed the animals. Chop stove wood."

"Like nothing's changed?" Jordy cried.

"I promised Pa we'd keep up the farm," Jake explained. "I expect you to do your part."

"Marty says maybe I should come to town and be his apprentice," Josh said. "I told Pa

I'd keep up my lessons. Ma wanted us to get educated."

"I can read as well as most," Jordy boasted. "I guess I could go. Saddle-making isn't so bad a trade, and I could keep up my writing helping with the post office."

"Nobody's going anywhere just yet," Jake told them. "We've got plenty of meal, chickens and hogs to eat, and game to shoot if there's need. Nobody's starving here."

"Jane Mary says Pa owes money," Jordy said, frowning. "Know how much, Jake?"

"No, but I've got some money saved back from working for the colonel," Jake explained. "We'll settle up any debts and start fresh. Don't you worry."

"We'll be all right, then?" Josh asked.

"Right as rain," Jake declared. "Solid as snow."

"Snow's not solid," Josh argued.

"Will be if it gets colder," Jake said, lifting the boy onto one shoulder. "Now, we've got work waiting, don't we?"

"Sure," Jericho agreed, grabbing an ax. "Coming, Jordy?"

"Just let me get a box for the slivers," Jordy replied.

"I know," Josh said, laughing. "Hogs and chickens."

Jake couldn't help grinning. Life was returning to normal, or at least as close to it as anyone could expect.

· · ·

Those last weeks of November and the December days that followed passed in a blur. When there weren't chores to tend, there were odd errands to run for Colonel Duncan or supplies to fetch from town. The family's few needs—molasses, sugar, coffee, and the like—were paid for by the silver dollars John Duncan provided. There were no frills, but Jake didn't notice his brothers missing them. Martin provided everyone with a pair of good cowhide boots for Christmas, and Jane Mary sewed poplin shirts and wool trousers for each of her brothers. Jake fashioned buckskin jackets from deer he shot in the wood lot, and he talked Colonel Duncan down to a bargain price on a pair of percussion rifles. For himself, Jake purchased a big-bore Sharps, and that allowed him to pass his old rifle along to Jericho.

"She's a beauty," Jericho said when Jake displayed his new rifle. It was as fine a gun as any man in Collin County carried, and Jake felt a hair taller with it in his hands.

"It's a buffalo gun," the colonel had told him. "You could drop an elephant with it if there was one around!"

The whole family gathered to celebrate Christmas, and a rare warmth filled the rooms of the dog-run cabin. Jane Mary took particular charge of Baby Joe, who was crawling around like a grasshopper of late, and Martin entertained his brothers-in-law with stories of his early days down south during the Texas fight for independence."

Betsy was oddly quiet, but Jake marked it down as missing his father. He himself felt the loss more than ever, for Christmas brought back recollections of other times and other years. Memories of his mother seemed to be everywhere, too.

"It's hard not to miss 'em, isn't it?" Jericho asked when he found Jake sitting beside their parents' graves on the lonely hillside Christmas night.

"Pa always said life was a fight," Jake explained. "Told me you had to stare it in the eye and scrap like a badger."

"It hasn't been so hard, though," Jericho observed. "We're doing passable well. Truth is, without Pa's schemes, we're even putting some money by."

"Oh?" Jake asked.

"Betsy sold off two hogs, you know. Brought in ten dollars cash."

"I didn't know," Jake confessed. "What'd she do with the money?"

"Paid some lawyer fellow from McKinney. Andrews, I think his name was."

"I never heard Pa talk about anybody named Andrews. Lawyer? What would Betsy need a lawyer for?"

"I guess it has to do with settling Pa's estate," Jericho explained. "Mr. Selwyn said they had some sort of meeting on it last week."

"I don't understand.

"Jake, don't you suppose Pa left the farm to us?" Jericho asked. "He would have made out a will, wouldn't he have? Can't all of it pass into Betsy's hands, can it? She could show us the door that way."

"Never thought on it," Jake admitted. "She's looked pretty perplexed lately. Maybe she's afraid we'd take the farm and send her off packing."

"She knows better," Jericho muttered. "No, it wouldn't be that."

Jake suddenly began to wonder, though. He refused to share his doubts, not wanting to mar the high spirits his brothers had found to share that Christmas, but once everyone took to their beds, he sat beside the fire, pondering matters.

Next morning, when Jane Mary herded the boys off to tend chores, Jake stayed behind.

"Leaving the chopping to Jericho?" Betsy asked good-naturedly as she cracked eggs in a bowl.

"Thought I might ask you a question," Jake explained.

"Go ahead," she urged. "I'm all ears."

"Jer said you paid money to some lawyer named Andrews," Jake said, frowning. "I never heard of him."

"You will," Betsy said, setting aside her work and gazing out the window. "He's handling your father's affairs."

"What's that mean, Betsy?"

"Joe had debts," she explained.

"He told me as much," Jake admitted. "He need a lawyer to pay his bills?"

"Jake, we're not talking about a bank draft

to buy seed. He invested a hundred dollars in that mill, for instance. He still owed money he borrowed to pay last year's taxes."

"How much is it altogether?" Jake asked, growing cold as he watched Betsy fidget.

"Almost seven hundred dollars," she said, sighing. "I have twenty-five dollars or so put by, and Jane Mary's offered forty. But—"

"Lord!" Jake cried. "I have around thirty saved. Seven hundred? We can't raise that kind of money selling all the animals and everything!"

"Damon Andrews has been delaying the creditors," Betsy explained. "They agreed to hold off so we could have Christmas here together, but—"

"They're taking the farm, huh?"

"Selling it, as I understand."

"Where will we live? What will we do?"

"I don't know," Betsy said, dropping her face into her hands. "Lord, I just don't know."

7

Jake's grandfather had once described Texas as a land full of savages and land thieves. Jake considered Grandpa Wetherby had left out the worst scalawags of all— lawyers! As Joe Wetherby's creditors descended on his family, one lawyer after another carved off a piece of the pie, until there was little left but heartache.

"The farm's gone," Damon Andrews explained. "Sold to pay the debts. I did my best for you, but top offer was two dollars an acre."

"You held onto the wood lot, then," Jake observed. "It's worth as much as the farm."

"You're right," Andrews noted. "We sold that at thirty an acre."

"There's nine hundred dollars right there," Betsy noted. "We should have been able to keep the farm."

"You're overlooking expenses and such," Andrews explained. "Taxes. Documents of transfer. I managed to clear a hundred thirty dollars for you."

"And the livestock?" Jake asked. "Horses? Wagon?"

"I insisted your mare is separate property, Jacob," the lawyer said. "The other stock went into the sale, I'm afraid. You retain the furniture, clothing."

"I guess we ought to be grateful, huh?" Jake cried. "We could be driven off naked, I guess."

"This isn't my doing," Andrews insisted. "It's your father took out these loans. The creditors were very patient, and they let you stay through Christmas. Moreover, Mr. Selwyn, your neighbor downstream, purchased the land. He's assured me you're welcome to stay in the house for now."

"Nice of him," Jake grumbled.

"It is," Betsy said, studying the pile of papers in front of her. "Frank Selwyn's been a good neighbor, and we have no reason to doubt that's changed."

"Si's been a good friend," Jericho added.

"And the little ones pass half the summer in the creek with us."

"I didn't mean to say different," Jake said, sighing. "It's just that without the animals and the land, the house doesn't do us much good."

"There's more," Andrews declared.

"What else?" Jake asked, throwing his arms in the air.

"Tell us," Betsy urged.

"There's the matter of the children," the lawyer said, gazing at Jake's brothers. "Naturally, Betsy, you retain guardianship over the baby, but these boys aren't your blood kin."

"No, they're mine," Jake declared.

"You're eighteen, Jacob," Andrews noted. "In Texas, a boy of sixteen's considered of age and not subject to the authority of the court."

"But we are, huh?" Jericho asked.

"That's true," Andrews replied. "Now, I've arranged a petition of adoption for you, Betsy. But there's certain to be questions over it."

"Wait a minute!" Jake shouted.

"Hold your water, young man," the lawyer suggested. "One thing at a time. Betsy, as surviving spouse you're entitled to half the value of the estate, sixty-five dollars. No judge will consider that sufficient support for four minor children."

"I'm their brother," Jake argued. "I'll look after them!"

"How?" Andrews asked. "Where would you live? You haven't got a job, Jacob, and your portion of the estate comes to what, ten dollars and change?"

"I won't have my brothers sent to some orphans' home," Jake vowed.

"You have kin," the lawyer observed.

"Jane Mary and Martin," Jordy pointed out. "We could stay with them."

"One of you, maybe," the lawyer agreed.

"I'm almost sixteen," Jericho declared. "I can go with Jake, and Jane Mary could look after Jordy and Josh for now."

"There's Uncle Dan, too," Jordy suggested. "And we've got family in Tennessee."

"Ma wanted us to stay together," Jake grumbled. "I promised Pa to take care of my brothers."

"It's not up to you, Jacob," the lawyer said, shaking his head. "Listen. What you want has very little value in court."

"Or anywhere else, I'd judge," Jake muttered.

"If you really want to try, I could draw up papers for you, but I have to tell you how slim the chances are. You'd be better advised to save your money and bide your time. Try to make a place for yourself. Then when your brothers come of age, they can choose for themselves."

"We'll be all right," Josh said, frowning. "It won't be so bad, making saddles."

"Don't give up just yet," Jake said, staring hard at the lawyer. "I'm not giving up without a fight."

As Andrews went on explaining the papers he had drawn up, Jake rose from the table and stormed out the door. He took only a few minutes to saddle Maizy, and shortly thereafter he was riding north into a stiff winter wind, bent on reaching Duncan's Station before noon. Soon a hard drizzle began to fall, and he found himself urging Maizy into a gallop.

Jake arrived at the station near frozen and out of breath.

Jefferson and Nathaniel took charge of Maizy, and Jake left the tormented horse in their able hands. He himself hurried inside the station. Miranda greeted him with a frown.

"Don't you know any better than to ride out into a norther?" she exclaimed. "You've got frost on your eyebrows, and your legs appear wet through. Skin out of those clothes while I find you some blankets."

"We know each other, but not near so well that I'll undress in front of you," Jake replied. "I came to see your pa, and I haven't got much time to waste."

"That you, Jacob Henry?" the colonel called from the warehouse.

"Colonel, I got trouble," Jake called, shivering.

John Duncan stepped through the doorway, looked Jake over, and shook his head.

"Pa, we'll be burying another Wetherby if he doesn't get out of those wet rags!" Miranda stormed.

"She's right, son," the colonel agreed, halting Jake with a motion of the hand. "Come along into the storeroom. You can dry yourself by the fire."

"First I've got to tell you—"

"I know all about it," Duncan said, waving Jake along.

"Colonel?"

"I've been expecting you," Duncan explained. "Was only a matter of time before the lawyers went to work. Get yourself dry, and we'll make us some plans. Strategy's the key to winning any fight."

"Yes, sir," Jake said, stepping over beside the fire and sitting on the hearth. As he pulled off his boots, Miranda set a kettle of hot tea beside him.

"Daughter, best you head on back to your chores," the colonel advised. "Wouldn't want Jacob Henry here to have a compromised woman on his hands. Boy's got trouble enough."

Jake managed half a smile. Miranda stomped off and slammed the door behind her.

"Tell me what they told you," the colonel suggested as Jake began peeling off soggy garments.

After stripping and wrapping a wool blanket around his frozen hide, Jake Wetherby did just that. Colonel Duncan listened to each detail. Occasionally he jotted something down on a sheet of paper. Otherwise he waited to speak until Jake finished.

"I admire you for wanting to take your brothers in hand," the colonel said, nodding. "But what would you do for them, son? The youngest two need a woman's hand more than rough living. I imagine a judge would let Jericho trail along with you—if you had any particular place to go."

"You're saying my brothers would be better off split up?" Jake cried. "Or with Betsy?"

"She's got enough worries," the colonel

71

declared. "No, with just the littlest one, she might find herself another husband."

"Jane Mary could take the boys for a time, but—"

"She and Martin have a hard go of it as is."

"You know an awful lot about all this," Jake observed.

"Some of us have looked into it," Duncan confessed. "A man feels a certain responsibility to his neighbors, you see."

"You're saying I shouldn't fight for my brothers?" Jake asked.

"No real point to it son. You won't win."

"You're awful sure."

"I know Judge Henderson, Jacob Henry. He's not a man to heap impossible burdens onto a boy's shoulders."

"I haven't been a boy for a long time," Jake argued. "Certainly not since Pa died."

"Jacob—"

"Jake. That's what folks call me now."

"Jake," the colonel said, grinning broadly, "I'm no one to consider an enemy, you know. But look at yourself. Skinny as a spring-born colt! Peaches have more fuzz on 'em than your body! You'll do well to look out for yourself."

"Pa had a hairy chest, and it didn't help him look after anybody," Jake grumbled. "I appreciate the warm fire, but I'd best head for town. Maybe somebody there can help me."

"There are lots of people eager to help, Jake," the colonel insisted. "You have to listen to them, though. I always figured Martin and Jane Mary would take Betsy and the baby in. Didn't concern myself about them."

"Go on," Jake urged.

"I suppose you know Franklin Selwyn purchased your pa's farm."

"The lawyer told us today."

"Frank's young brother-in-law and young Jer are close."

"Sure, I know that," Jake admitted. "Si was about the first friend we had when we came out from Tennessee."

"Do you also know Frank's filed a guardianship paper with Judge Henderson."

"For Jericho?"

"And the younger ones, too," Colonel Duncan explained.

"He's got a houseful of little ones already," Jake objected. "What would he want with my brothers?"

"His boys are small, Jake. With those new sections, Si's bound to need some help."

"Jer wouldn't mind partnering up with Si," Jake observed. "The two of them make for a lot of mischief, but I'd guess Mr. Selwyn can tolerate it. Always has. You figure Jordy and Josh would be better off there than with me?"

"Don't you, son?"

"Suppose so," Jake admitted. "They'd be able to finish their schooling."

"Beats crafting saddles, don't you think?"

"Colonel, all this is falling on my head like summer hail. I don't know what to make of it."

"That's how things happen sometimes, Jake," Colonel Duncan observed. "You could still fight it, and I suspect we could work out a way for you to win, too. But don't you figure your brothers might have the best part of the bargain if you let 'em go along to Frank Selwyn?"

Jake hung his head and began rubbing the last of the moisture out of his flesh. Clearly the colonel was right. The boys wouldn't be split up, and Franklin Selwyn was sure to provide a guiding hand.

"Then all that's left to sort out is what I'm going to do," Jake mumbled at last.

"There's plenty of work to be had by a fine, enterprising young man like yourself."

"Such as?"

"What is it you favor doing, son? Can't be running errands from here to town!"

"I like horses, and I'm a good shot. You figure I might be fit for the army?"

"No, you're not half addled enough," Duncan said, laughing. "Haven't seen you drunk once, Jake. Nor in jail. Good honest sort like yourself wouldn't get past the first muster."

"Then what, Colonel?"

"Well, the stage line hires drivers on occasion."

"Figure me for an iron-bottom old cuss like Jerry Platt?" Jake asked.

"No, you don't cuss half good enough," the colonel said, scratching his head. "Too fair-haired to make a decent stable hand."

"You hire men to move freight."

"I do, Jake, but you'd never be content with moving boxes around."

"You do have something in mind, though,"

Jake said, spotting a glimmer in Duncan's eye. "Tell me about it, won't you? I've had my fair share of disappointment today. A helping of hope would be particular welcome."

"Might be at that," Duncan agreed. "Ever pass through Denton County, Jake?"

"Once or twice," Jake explained. "Just the corner of it. I helped chase down some maverick cows once."

"Well, it's chasing another kind of critter I've got in mind."

"Horses," Jake said, nodding. "Mustangs."

"Best cash crop in Texas," Duncan boasted. "Man can have enough cornmeal and coffee, but horses are always in high demand. I know a place where they run thick as fleas on a lazy hound."

"Mustang Flats," Jake declared. "I've heard of the place."

"Miles of hills and creeks, with no people to bother you. No towns. No roads."

"No lawyers," Jake added.

"Nothing but wild horses. It's not easy work, running 'em down and throwing a rope over their heads. And afterward there's the breaking! Lord, it's a vexation beyond measure. But when you finish, you've got an animal you can ride to tomorrow and back. Even the sorriest-looking animal in the herd will bring ten, fifteen dollars."

"All clear profit, too," Jake observed.

"I plan to take a dozen men up there, Jake, and split the profits with the outfit even up, fifty-fifty. You'd make money."

"I'm your man, Colonel. Only if it's such

a fine notion, why aren't there crews up there all the time? Why ask me to join you when there are full-grown men in need of making a living?"

"Other bunches have gone up there, Jake, but a lot of 'em haven't come back. Leastwise not with their hair."

"Indians?"

"Comanches. Kiowas. The very worst sort. They're born horse thieves, and they take it ill we chase after their horses."

"Their horses?"

"Any critter not branded and papered is theirs, to their way of thinking," Duncan explained. "Truth be told, they probably consider anything with four legs their personal property."

"I've heard tales of Comanches," Jake confessed, shuddering. "Some murdered a family out on Rowlett Creek."

"Fifteen years back or so," Duncan said, shaking his head. "To hear the stories, you'd judge it was yesterday.

"Hasn't been that long since somebody's been killed up at Mustang Flats, though, or you wouldn't find it hard to assemble an outfit."

"True enough, Jake," the colonel admitted. "I'll agree there's danger, but the reward's fair to middling. What do you say? Coming along?"

"I don't see I've got a lot of choices," Jake replied. "I trust you to keep us out of tight places, Colonel."

"Do my best, Jake. You stay here tonight and think on it some more. Then ride on home and look after your brothers till Judge Henderson convenes his court. I don't expect to head north before March."

"What will I do till then?"

"I suspect we can find a place for you in the stable loft, and Miranda's never shy about finding work for me to do. I'll turn you over to her."

"Thanks, Colonel," Jake said, offering his hand.

"You'll do your part, Jake. Like I said before, I won't be doing you a favor. Just offering you pay for a task well done."

Maybe so, Jake thought. But that was a whole lot more than anybody else was doing!

8

Judge Clark Henderson convened his circuit court in the county seat of McKinney, some fifteen miles to the north. Franklin Selwyn allowed Jake the use of the old wagon to haul his family there. The judge was a tall, lanky gentleman with dark brown hair giving way to gray around the temples. An Alabaman by birth, there were traces of the deep South in his speech and manner. Jake hoped maybe the judge would display particular consideration for a band of Tennesseans.

Actually, Judge Henderson barely noticed the Wetherbys. Lawyer Andrews presented some papers, but before he could argue their merit, the judge waved him quiet.

"This matter appears settled," Judge Henderson declared. "Don't give me a headache with a lot of gibberish, Damon. There's no money to be made talking in my court. The minor child Joseph Wetherby, Junior, is to stay with his mother. The other minors are placed in the guardianship of Franklin Selwyn of Collin County. Estate is settled as recommended. Next case," the judge concluded, rapping his gavel.

"Don't we get to talk?" Jericho asked, rising to his feet.

"Don't you agree with the settlement, son?" Judge Henderson asked.

"I'd as soon go with Jake," Jericho declared. "I don't need anybody guarding me."

"No?" the judge asked, grinning. "Well, I suspect it won't hurt you to have Mr. Selwyn see to your schooling. And those britches hang too loose. They appear to me in need of filling out."

"Jake?" Jericho asked, turning toward his older brother.

"Isn't anything else to do," Jake explained. "And it won't be forever."

"Sure," Jericho muttered, turning away.

Jake accompanied his brothers outside the courthouse, and for a time the four brothers sat silently. Jane Mary and Betsy stood ten feet away, tending to the baby.

"It's not fair," Jordy grumbled. "We lose Ma, then Pa. Now the farm's gone, too."

"You knew all about it, didn't you, Jake?" Jericho asked, smoothing down a rebellious strand of strawberry-blond hair. "How come you never said anything?"

"Jake?" Josh asked with widening eyes.

"The colonel told me," Jake explained. "You know how I wanted it. We could have made a go of the farm, but without the house, with no land to work—"

"We could maybe work shares," Jordy suggested.

"And how would you do that and go to school?" Jake asked. "We all promised Ma you'd finish your education."

"What'll you do, Jake?" Jordy asked. "Judge didn't say you'd go to the Selwyns."

"I'm eighteen," Jake explained.

"You'd be welcome anyway," Frank Selwyn said, walking over with Silas Garrett.

"Seems to me you've got enough of my family to worry over," Jake observed. "Colonel Duncan's invited me to go mustanging in March. Meanwhile I figure to work at the station, cutting wood and doing odd jobs."

"We could still go hunting sometimes," Jordy said, frowning. "Fishing, too. Swim some when it warms up."

"And you'd be welcome to stop by for dinner whenever you have the chance," Selwyn added. "I don't mean to steal your family away, Jake. Just help 'em along."

"I know that," Jake said. "I appreciate it. It's nobody's fault, what's happened. Just another turn in the road."

"Jake?" Josh asked.

"Yeah, I know. It tears at me, too, little brother," Jake confessed as the eleven-year-old leaned against his side. "I'll be missing your pranks, you know."

"I know," Josh mumbled.

"You'll all of you mind your manners," Jake urged.

"Sure," Jordy said, leading Josh toward the wagon.

"Jer, it's up to you to look after 'em now," Jake said.

"Guess it's my turn," Jericho replied, mustering a faint smile. "I'm carrying the Kentuck rifle now."

"Don't worry so much over them you neglect Amy Anders," Jake whispered.

"Wetherbys always find time for the important things," Jericho assured his brother. "You watch out for that Miranda Duncan, though. She's the sort to hog-tie a man and force a promise out of him."

"That or brain him with a skillet lid," Jake noted, laughing at the thought. He then gripped Jericho's hands. Jericho held on for a bit before letting go. Jake stepped over and rested a hand on Josh's shoulder. Jordy flashed a smile.

" 'Bye, Jake," Josh said when Jericho climbed atop the wagon.

"You're coming along, aren't you?" Jordy asked.

"No, I think I'll go back with Jane Mary," Jake explained. "Saying good-bye once is hard enough."

"Twice'd be nigh impossible," Jordy observed.

Jake nodded his agreement, and Jericho urged the mules into motion. Frank Selwyn and Si Garrett mounted their ponies and followed ten yards behind.

"Coming along, Jake?" Jane Mary called.

"No, I think I'll walk," Jake told her. "I need some time to myself."

"I don't know that I find much favor in that notion," Jane Mary argued. "It's gone and turned cool."

"You've got enough to worry about," Jake replied, gazing at Betsy and the baby. "Time I took charge of myself."

She started to object, but Jake had already turned and started away. She followed him in the buggy for a time, then gave up when he swung west from the main road. Jake continued alone. The solitude near choked him, but what else could he do? It was best gotten used to.

The walk itself was a balm. As he wove his way across the deserted hillsides and forded familiar creeks, he was reminded of better days, times full of laughter and adventure. Only when he splashed across Spring Creek and approached the dog-run cabin that was no longer home did his step waver.

"Maizy girl," he called to the speckled mare.

Maizy leaned her head over the corral rail, and Jake patted her nose. He then slid the rails back and led the horse toward the barn. Jake retrieved his gear from the tack room and slowly, deliberately, saddled Maizy. Finally he walked over to the deserted house and collected his blanket roll and a flour sack stuffed with his odds and ends of clothing. He made a second and final trip to fetch the Sharps rifle.

After tying everything in place, he mounted the mare and headed west.

Jake didn't ride far. He stopped at the base of the knoll where his mother and father were buried. Slowly, silently, he rolled off the horse and approached the two lonely markers.

"Ma, Pa, I did what I could, but it wasn't much," he whispered. "Jane Mary's sure to see the baby's looked after, and the boys are over at the Selwyn place. I'm off to Duncan's Station now. Hope to make my fortune as a mustanger."

It wasn't what his mother had hoped or his father expected, but Jake deemed it for the best. As he returned to his horse and mounted up, he took a last glance back toward the house.

Leaving Tennessee was easy, he told himself. This is what hard is.

He then nudged Maizy into a trot. It was time to leave the past behind.

Those next few weeks at Duncan's Station weren't altogether bad. By and by Jake grew accustomed to Miranda's sharp tongue, and he found Nathaniel and Jefferson to be full of stories.

"Got to say, for a white man, you don't make such bad company, Jake Wetherby," Nathaniel told him one evening when Jake returned to the station with a fresh-killed deer.

"I take that for high praise," Jake replied. "You aren't known for handing out compliments as a rule."

"Takes after the colonel," Jefferson said, laughing. "Now, if you can get that man to take a shine to you, you'll likely be able to talk Saint Peter out of the keys to the pearly gates!"

Sometimes Jake suspected there was a fair measure of truth to that observation.

"Pull on that rope, Jacob Henry!" Colonel Duncan shouted one morning when they were trying to lower a bale of hay from the barn loft. "Pull!"

"I'm trying my best!" Jake screamed in reply as he fought to keep his grip on the rope. "It's too heavy for one man to manage."

"Man?" the colonel cried. "That what I've got here? I do believe I've seen stray dogs outweighed you, boy!"

"Maybe that's who you should take mustanging, then!" Jake barked as he swung the bale out from the loft and tried to lower it gently. The dead weight overpowered him, though, and the rope tore his hands as it escaped his grip. The bale landed with a thud, disturbing the horses stabled nearby. Jefferson and Nathaniel had a battle on their hands quieting them.

"Good-for-nothing, addle-brained fool!" Colonel Duncan hollered. "Near dropped that bale on my head!"

"Sorry, Colonel," Jake said, wincing from the pain of his blistered hands.

"Told you to let me help," Jefferson grumbled.

"You go and forget who you are?" Duncan asked. His face flushed scarlet, and Jake feared Jefferson might feel the toe of a well-placed boot.

"I know I got fifty pounds on that boy up

in that loft," Jefferson muttered. "And on a good day I need Nat's help to move them hay bales. Lucky you didn't go and flip that boy right up onto the moon!"

"You never talked like that around Luke Berry!" Duncan complained. "He would've whipped you white."

"I'd welcome that, Colonel," Jefferson said, laughing as he clipped the rawhide bands holding the bale together. "Thataway I wouldn't be anybody's slave no more."

"Slaves." Duncan growled. "Trouble. Luke warned me not to feed you beef."

"Don't look to me that it's much of a tonic," Nathaniel observed as he climbed the ladder to the loft. "I don't believe Jake's been eating at all, and he's sassier'n any stable boy you ever had."

"Colonel, I'm sorry," Jake said as Nathaniel painted the torn hands with salve. "Guess you got a poor bargain when you took me in."

"Didn't cost no thousand dollars," Jefferson mumbled.

"No, wasn't as big a mistake as when I took you on, Jefferson!" Duncan declared. "Are those hands bad?"

"They still attached," Nathaniel noted. "Won't be working hay for a time."

"Well, get along to the station, then, and have Miranda look at them," the colonel said, waving toward the door. "I guess we can finish here without you."

"Did before you come along," Nathaniel said, hiding a grin. "Watch those sores now, hear?"

"Sure," Jake said, nodding as he descended the ladder.

"Should've said it was too much for you," Colonel Duncan said when he gazed at Jake's hands. "Rope burn's enough to lay up a man weeks."

"I won't charge you any day I don't work," Jake grumbled. "And I'll pay for my keep."

"Wasn't asking for any favors," Duncan said, motioning Jake outside. "I'll decide what's owed whom!"

Jake shook his head and stumbled outside. As he approached the station house, he wasn't certain whether he was angrier at himself for losing control of the bale or at the colonel for the hard words.

"Best hurry and get yourself grown tall, Jake Wetherby," he told himself. "There's no respecting a runt around this place!"

Jake was in sore need of comfort just then— or at least a trace of sympathy. He hoped to get some of one or the other from Miranda, but she disappointed him.

"Lord, Jake, what'll you do next?" she grumbled. "Get your hands out to the pump and wash that salve off. Just what I need with two stages due today. A nurse's chores tacked on!"

"Don't bother yourself over me," Jake insisted. "I'll head into town and get Jane Mary to tend them."

"Figure to hold Maizy's reins in your teeth, I suppose?" she barked. "Do as I say. Now!"

He complied with her orders, and when he

returned, she painted the burns with ointment and wrapped them in gauze.

"Thanks," he whispered afterward.

"I hope they heal fast," she replied. "I'm low on stove wood."

Some days were better than others, but most were a mixture of feuding and open warfare.

"I can't exactly understand it," Jake told his brothers when they sat together on the creek bank near Harrison's Crossroads the first week of March. "The colonel was downright considerate when I went to see him after Pa died."

"Hard as Pa, huh?" Josh asked.

"I just thought Pa was mean," Jake grumbled. "Why, the colonel'd rather chew a chicken bone up than spit it out and admit there was one to begin with!"

"People can turn on you," Jericho observed. "I warned you about that Miranda, too. She's got notions, Jake."

"They're all after husbands," Jordy said, nodding his head as if knowing all about it at thirteen.

"Looks like Betsy's got herself one," Jericho grumbled. "Maybe you could move in with Jane Mary now, Jake."

"Betsy's getting married?" Jake asked. "Pa's scarce in the ground!"

"She wouldn't want to waste a chance like this," Jericho declared. "She didn't profit much by marrying Pa, but Doc Springfield's rich."

"Doc?" Jake cried. "He's got four little ones. She'd be a fool to—"

"There were four of us," Jordy said, grinning. "Doc's got a maid and a cook, too. I expect Betsy'll have some easy living ahead of her."

"It's not respectful," Jake grumbled.

"That's what Jane Mary thought, too," Jericho explained. "But she's come around. Thinks Baby Joe needs a father."

"He's got brothers," Jake argued.

"Sure, but where will we be when he's my age?" Josh asked. "Chasing ponies or off hunting buffalo, most likely. I don't hold it against Betsy for wanting an easier life."

"No, she was a middling stepmother," Jordy agreed.

"Anyway," Jericho suggested, "you could partner up with Martin at the saddle shop or maybe run the post office. Jane Mary'd be as bossy as Miranda, but she wouldn't be trying to marry you."

"Wouldn't abide much independence, either," Jordy said, laughing. "Me, I'd take some burned hands and harsh words over a broom-bashing, sharp-tongued sister any day!"

"You settling in with the Selwyns all right?" Jake asked, changing the subject.

"They've been real good to us," Jericho explained. "Frank's added a room onto the house for us, and Si's always finding fresh mischief to share. The little sprouts aren't too troublesome, and Miz Selwyn's as good a cook as Ma."

"Almost," Josh added.

"You all of you look better," Jake noted. In truth, they were growing taller and filling out just fine. Their clothes were free of tears, and they wore good shoes. Jake was ashamed to compare his own ragged buckskin jacket and faded trousers.

"You'll have to stop by and share supper sometime," Jordy said, scrambling to his feet. "You've been invited all along, you know."

"I'd just be an extra burden," Jake declared.

"Guess we best get along home now," Jericho said, rising. "Miz Selwyn worries, you know, and we've got chores."

"I've got obligations myself," Jake told them. He stood and watched as they snaked their way homeward. He envied them the sense of belonging they had acquired. And he knew he would feel even colder sleeping alone in the loft that night.

9

That next week, John Duncan began assembling his mustanging outfit. The first to arrive was Casper Winfrey. Casper stood six-foot-four in stocking feet, and he was a comical sight on a horse. He didn't look to be too familiar with water, and Miranda refused to allow him in her dining room.

"You'll wash first!" she insisted.

Casper preferred to take his meals outdoors.

Luther Gaines appeared later that same

day. Lute was a wiry boy of sixteen who stood a whisker shy of five-foot-six. Jake struck up a kinship with the boy straight off, for Lute was a natural-born clown. If he wasn't pranking Miranda, he'd be grinning or coaxing a tune out of his mouth organ.

"Lute's also the laziest body this side of Hades," Miranda observed. He was so good-natured, though, even she found it impossible to hold a grudge against him.

Bob Sturgess and Ham McCullough were freight handlers who rode down from Preston to join the expedition. They were both in their early thirties, sour-faced and stand-offish. They rarely paid notice to Jake, and when they did, it was to find fault with him.

"I suppose they know horses, though," Jake told Lute.

"Wouldn't want to bet money on it," Lute replied. "They don't look too easy in the saddle, and they ain't built for sitting a horse."

In contrast, Tommy Carmichael had served five years in the Second U.S. Cavalry. He wasn't yet twenty-five, and most days he didn't look that. Put a rifle in his hands, though, and he went snake-eyed and cold.

"Seen that scar on his side?" Lute asked. Jake shook his head, and Lute explained how a surgeon had dug a Comanche arrowhead out of Tommy two summers back.

"He's only fair with a rope," Lute noted, "but he's steady. Hates Comanches. If any come calling, I plan to settle in beside Tommy. Yes, sir, you can count on that."

The last to join the company were Ed and Tyler Raymond. Ed was closing in on fifty, Jake suspected, and looked even older. A twice-broken hip made riding difficult and walking any distance nigh impossible.

"He's come along to cook," Lute explained. "Does that fair, too."

Tyler was Ed's boy. At twelve, Ty was no bigger than Jake's brother Josh. Freckled and sad, the boy kept to his father's shadow.

"I tried to teach him to play cards once," Lute said, shaking his head. "Boy's got no number sense, and he can't read. Truth is, I don't know there's much purpose to him being alive. Give him a bucket of water, and he'll spill two-thirds before he manages to walk ten feet!"

Jake wrote it off to shyness, though.

"He was lively enough before his ma died," Miranda explained when she helped Jake load supplies in a short-bed wagon. "Never's been the same since."

Jake felt a certain kinship for Tyler, figuring they were both orphans of a sort.

"Ah, I got no folks, neither," Lute remarked. "It's not so much to slow a fellow down. Ty just needs to muster some gumption and dive into things."

Instead, Tyler sat in the back of the supply wagon his father was to drive, whining and whittling.

"We're some outfit, eh?" Jake asked as he rode beside Colonel Duncan north and west into Denton County.

"Mighty slim pickings this year," the colonel

grumbled. "I got the leavings swept out of saloons or run off farms."

"Figure we can still make a cash crop off those mustangs?" Jake asked.

"There's a chance," Duncan replied. "Not a good one, though. But if it doesn't hail, and the Comanches leave us be... well, we could do all right by ourselves."

Jake was counting on it. He'd spent the last of his silver dollars buying a pair of good wool blankets. If this enterprise failed, Colonel Duncan was as apt as not to send him packing. Penniless, too.

"Oh, we'll do just fine," Lute boasted as he trotted alongside. "Don't you take the colonel to heart. He's more worry than wisdom."

"Lute," Jake asked, "just what do you do when you aren't chasing mustangs or philosophizing?"

"Oh, I play my harmonica at the saloons in Dallas," Lute explained. "Carry the mail sometimes. Wash windows, patch roofs, paint barns... whatever needs doing."

"How'd the colonel come to ask you along?"

"Well, I suppose he thinks he owes my pa," Lute explained.

"Were they friends?" Jake asked.

"No, I wouldn't say that. Pa was a road agent down around Waco. Back when the colonel was riding with the Rangers, Pa tried to rob a freighter. Colonel Duncan chased him down and saw him hung."

"Lute?"

"Can't blame the colonel for doing his job," Lute argued. "Anyway, he drops off a few dollars sometimes. Seeing I've grown bigger, he asked me to chase down some prairie ponies. Knows I take after Pa some. I'm a devil on a horse, Jake!"

As if to prove it, Lute slapped his horse into a gallop. To his dismay, it took Jake a quarter hour to catch him after he nudged Maizy into motion.

"If you two've got so much energy, ride along ahead and see if you can spy any horses!" Colonel Duncan shouted.

"Yes, sir!" Lute answered, swinging his way north. Jake followed.

They were only two days scouring the hilly country that made up eastern Denton County. Beyond, in the flatlands on either side of two creeks, lay the country known as Mustang Flats. It came by its name honestly, for Jake counted close to two hundred ponies there. Lute rode ahead and returned with word there were even more on the far side of a nearby hill.

"We'll start with these here," Colonel Duncan declared. He then located a work camp inside a bend in the nearest creek. Sturgess and McCullough repaired a broken-down work corral while Casper Winfrey led Lute, Tommy Carmichael, and Jake after the horses.

"See that bog there?" Casper said, taking care to skirt it.

"Yes, sir," Jake noted.

"We're going to run those horses into it. Once they get snagged in the mud, we rope the best ones and drag 'em along to the corral. Understand?"

"Nothing to it," Carmichael replied.

"Best we fan out," Casper instructed. "Wave your hat, a blanket, whatever you got handy. That'll start 'em running. The trick's to force 'em into the bog. Then the serious work can begin."

Jake didn't understand the truth of those words until later.

"Come on, Maizy girl," he whispered as Casper waved him past Lute to the far left. Tommy Carmichael swung to the right at the same time. It was Casper who started the horses running, though, when he slapped his hat against his knee and uttered a banshee cry.

"Ayy-hyy-ooooh!" the bowlegged mustanger screamed.

"Yahhh!" Lute howled.

"Run, boys, run!" Jake shouted.

And run those ponies did. A coal-black stallion turned back and led one band between Jake and Casper and on to safety. The others fled in panic, though, and most soon splashed into the bog. Trapped by the mud, they made easy targets for a wrangler's rope.

"Take that pinto there, boy," Casper shouted, and Jake formed a loop in his lariat and tossed it nimbly over the mustang's neck. Then, wrapping the opposite end around his saddle horn, Jake began pulling the mustang from the mud.

At first all went just fine. The pinto was just as happy to escape the bog as Jake was to let him. Once out of the mud, though, it was a whole different story. The pinto reared up on its hind legs, snorted furiously, and gave a violent tug on the rope. Jake's saddle had never been the best in Texas, and the strain tore the horn right from the leather. Jake managed to catch the loose end of the rope and hold on, but the pinto, sensing freedom, pulled him right out of his stirrups and deposited him face first in the mud.

"Well, howdy, Jake!" Lute called as he rode past dragging a black mare with white speckles across its flanks. "Looks to me like you lost that pinto."

"Not yet," Jake muttered, spitting out mud as he got to his feet. The rope lay only a foot away, and Jake grabbed it, whistled Maizy over, and remounted. This time he dug his toes deeper in the stirrups and wrapped the rope around his waist and Maizy's neck. The pinto tried the same trick but made little progress. Jake gradually drew the rope in and began driving the pinto along toward the work corral.

Once the pinto was safely confined, Jake returned to the bog. Before nightfall he roped three other horses, including what even Colonel Duncan declared to be the pick of the bunch—a big sandy-haired stallion.

"Yes, sir, he's a looker," Lute observed. "Make a fair mount for anybody."

"Not till he's broken," Casper muttered. "And that ain't going to be easy by the look of him. Fiery-eyed, I'd say. You won't bend that one's head by whistling."

Jake now had a chance to see how a real mustanger earned his pay. A stubble-cheeked boy might throw a rope over a pony, but it took a mixture of snake oil salesman, polecat, and mule to coax a mustang into accepting a saddle. Casper employed every trick to gentle those horses. Some he confused by dropping flour sacks over their eyes so they couldn't see. Others he offered sugar and sweet grass to curry their cooperation. He half fooled the pinto by tying a blanket roll onto its back so it would get used to the weight.

"Mostly he outthinks those fool ponies," Lute observed. "Casper smells like a horse, whines like one, and even looks like one most mornings."

But whatever you said about Casper Winfrey, you had to admit he knew horses.

Jake tried his hand at breaking the sandy-haired stallion. Big Sandy, Jake called the horse, but it didn't take kindly to the name or Jake either one. That horse tossed Jake around so many times it was dizzying. Twice Jake was flung hard against a corral post, and once Big Sandy near trampled him.

"Sandy?" Lute cried. "That's no name for him."

Surprisingly, little Tyler Raymond offered a suggestion.

"Call him Demon," the boy said. "Look at his eyes. He's a devil if ever you saw one shaped like a horse."

The next time Jake climbed atop the stallion, he whispered, "All right, Demon, do your worst. I'll only come back and fight you all over again."

Five minutes later Jake was sprawled in the dust, but he didn't give up. By week's end he was sitting on Demon's back.

Colonel Duncan, Casper, Sturgess, and McCullough set off to rope another batch shortly thereafter, leaving Lute and Jake to nurse their bruises and work the rough off the horses already in the corral. Tommy Carmichael stayed to keep a watch over the camp.

"It's only sensible to take precautions," Lute said as he and Jake began exercising the mustangs. "Casper says he thought he saw someone spying at us across the creek."

"Thieves?" Jake asked warily.

"Worse," Lute answered. "Indians.

"Oh, they aren't half the bother folks make out," Jake said, grinning. "I remember a time just after we came out here from Tennessee. I was out with my brothers, collecting kindling for the stove. I heard horses splashing in the creek, so I turned to have a look. Were thirty Indians riding straight for our house. Near naked every one of them, too, and carrying bows and rifles. Ma let go a scream, and my brothers raced off into the trees, howling that we were about to be massacred. Those Indians sat on their horses, staring as Ma hung up washing. Then she stepped inside, fetched some sugar candy she made from cane, and began passing it around. Every one of those Indians had a sweet tooth. They left Ma some beaded moccasins and let loose a whoop or two. Then they rode off."

"It's a fair enough story," Lute admitted, "but I'd bet they weren't Comanches. I don't think the Comanche's been born who much liked a white man. Mostly they steal horses and burn barns, but they can scalp you if they've a mind. Or shoot arrows into you like they did Tommy."

"You figure they'd take interest in us?"

"Not us especially, but they're fond of horses."

"Well, they'd not get much of a bargain in Demon here," Jake said, laughing.

Lute started to reply, then froze. He released the rope guiding the two horses he was leading around the corral and turned white as a fresh-washed sheet.

"Lute?" Jake asked.

Before Lute could answer, Jake was shaken by a highpitched whine.

"Maizy!" Jake shouted, abandoning the mustangs and racing for the supply wagon. Maizy was grazing just beyond, or had been. At that moment a half-naked dark-haired boy no bigger than Tyler Raymond was fighting to drag the mare away.

"Leave her be!" Jake shouted as he ducked under the corral rails and raced for his horse. The young raider released Maizy and strung his bow. Before he could notch an arrow, though, Jake lowered a shoulder and knocked him flat. The boy lost his bow but managed to scramble away while Jake grabbed his Sharps rifle from his blankets.

"Get to cover, you boys!" Tommy Carmichael shouted. The ex-cavalryman had taken shelter on a slight rise studded with boulders. Jake dug out a cartridge box and headed that way.

He got only a few feet before stumbling over something soft and mushy. His left hand touched a small, leathery object. Holding it up, Jake saw it was a bloody ear.

"Lord, no," Jake cried as he fought to get to his feet. Beside him lay the mutilated remains of Ed Raymond. Jake staggered a step, then dropped to his knees and retched.

"Get hold of yourself," Lute pleaded, grabbing Jake's arm. "Come on. We got to get to cover."

Already Tommy's rifle was barking, and a chorus of whoops rose from the far side of the wagon as the raiders broke down the corral rails.

"Damned Comanches!" Tommy shouted, standing and waving his rifle at them. "Come up and fight!" he yelled, along with some words Jake had never heard. They must have been Comanche, for they drew an instant response. Three of the raiders climbed atop ponies and galloped toward the rise.

"Get down, boys!" Tommy shouted. Jake and Lute dropped like stones, and the rifle barked. The lead Comanche rolled off the side of the pinto.

"Jake, you ever fire that rifle of yours?" Lute asked.

"Not at anybody shooting back," Jake muttered as he raced on toward the rocks.

Tommy, meanwhile, managed to reload and clip a second rider. Jake got the Sharps loaded and fired at the third, but the shot was hopelessly wide of the mark. Lute fired off a handgun, too, but the rider might have run all three of them down if his horse hadn't stumbled.

"Fool," Jake said as he fought to control his fingers and get the Sharps reloaded. "He went and climbed on Demon. Nobody stays atop that stallion for long!"

Tommy fired again then, and the Comanche was further discouraged when the ball shattered his bow. Howling defiantly as they carried off their wounded comrade, the raiders were content to take horses and leave the three cowering mustangers on the rise.

Later, when Colonel Duncan and the others returned, they discovered little Tyler Raymond hadn't been as lucky. He lay near the creek with a water bucket in his hand, staring at the sky with wide, startled eyes. A strip of his hair had been cut away, and one of the raiders had taken his boots, shirt, and trousers.

"They appear to've taken pity on him," Lute observed as he bent down and closed the boy's eyes. "Didn't cut him much."

"Quick-killed," Tommy agreed. "Comanches can be downright generous where fools are concerned."

"Generous?" Jake asked. "They killed him."

"They can do worse," Tommy said, shuddering. "Pray you never see it, Jake boy. You won't sleep through a night ever again."

"I wish I'd gotten to know him," Jake said, rubbing his eyes. "He was almost friendly last night at supper."

"I don't imagine he held it against you, son," Colonel Duncan said, frowning. "He was on the simple side."

"Now he's simple dead," Jake mumbled.

"Best get a spade and cover him up," the colonel said, nodding to Sturgess. "Put him with his father."

"Sure, Colonel," Sturgess agreed. "What about them horses?"

"We worked too hard to break 'em," Jake said, staring angrily past the creek to where the Comanches had vanished. "We go and get 'em back."

"You're crazy, boy," McCullough declared. "I'm getting out of here with my hair."

"Devil take the horses," Sturgess agreed. "I'm with Mac."

"I never let anybody take anything off me without a fight," Lute said, swallowing hard as he stepped over and stood shoulder to shoulder with Jake Wetherby. "Colonel?"

"What do you say to the likes of these two, Tom?" Duncan asked. "Spank 'em or join 'em?"

"I never was much for giving away my property, either," Tommy answered. "Let's tend our dead and set out tonight on a little horse-raiding of our own. You with me, Colonel?"

"Might as well get myself scalped here as someplace else," Duncan declared. "Be a thing to remember, stealing horses off a Comanche!"

"Sure," Tommy agreed. "If we live to tell it.

10

By the time the Raymonds were laid to rest, Colonel Duncan had begun to reconsider. The hurried departure of Sturgess and McCullough had left the camp oddly empty. There was no hiding how pitifully few of them were left.

"Those Comanches are sure to be halfway to the Red River by now," Colonel Duncan argued. "We've lost a week's work, but there are plenty of horses left to rope. You can't go making war on Comanches."

"I can," Tommy insisted. "Anyhow, it seems to me it's them started it."

"This is their country," Casper declared.

"Maybe so," Lute grumbled, "but those horses were ours!"

"What about Tyler?" Jake asked, staring hard at Casper and the colonel, each in turn. "You figure we should just forget about him and his pa?"

"We do, and you'll find wranglers hard to come by next time you head for Mustang Flats," Tommy said. "You say those Comanches headed north. Why? More likely they're camped close by, waiting for us to get some ponies ready for 'em."

"Colonel?" Jake asked.

"We'll understand if you call it quits," Tommy said, scowling. "You got Miranda to consider, and a good business. We three got nothing to lose. Where I come from, though, you stand your ground and take care of your partners. Otherwise you've got nothing at all. So if these two young fools are up to the ride, I believe we'll have a try at getting those horses back."

"Casper?" Duncan asked.

"Be best if somebody stays and watches the camp," Casper replied. "If you're of a mind to stay, I'll go. You want to go, I'll stay."

"Keep a fire burning high," the colonel suggested. "Guess it's right we punish those varmints. Maybe Tyler wasn't much use, but Ed was a fine cook. They're hard to come by."

"Glad you're with us, Colonel," Jake declared. "With you leading, we'll make out just fine."

"No, Tommy's the Indian fighter," Duncan grumbled. "Let him get you killed."

They left shortly thereafter. Four men didn't make up much of an army, especially when two were only half grown, but Jake figured they had an edge. They were too mad to be afraid, and the memory of Ed Raymond's butchered corpse drove them on. Tommy picked up the Comanches' trail on the far side of the creek, and he followed it warily. A little short of dusk Tommy pointed to two gray spirals of smoke on the far side of a nearby hill.

"That'll be the camp," he explained. "Let's turn up that ravine and sneak in on them. Keep yourselves and your mounts quiet now. I want to hit 'em suddenlike, around dusk."

"Not too sudden, though, hear?" Lute pleaded. "I'd rather them be the surprised ones."

Colonel Duncan shook his head in dismay. The closer they got to the raiders' camp, the less eager to charge the mustangers became. Nevertheless, Tommy went on ahead to scout the camp. He returned shortly and scratched an outline of the hillside in the dirt.

"They've got their horses here," he explained, pointing to the base of the hill. "Their lodges are up in the trees and hard to get at. Best we hit the horses and run 'em off quick. Leave 'em afoot."

"You'll need a diversion," Duncan observed. "Otherwise the guards will be on us. How many did you see?"

"Three boys minding the ponies," Tommy answered. "Up in the camp there's another dozen."

"They'd sure see something burning," Jake suggested. "We could set their tipis afire."

"Sure, they'd notice that all right," Tommy agreed. "Don't you figure they might see a man waving a torch, though?"

"Don't plan to use a torch," Jake explained. "The grass here's so dry a spark'll get it going. I've got my flints with me, and I'll just set a little blaze."

"Even if they miss seeing you, they'll smell the fire," Tommy objected.

"You want 'em to chase me, don't you?" Jake asked. "I run fair, and I'll have Maizy tied and waiting. They won't catch me."

"He's right, Colonel," Lute agreed. "I've chased him. He's quicker'n a jackrabbit."

"We won't be able to help," Duncan emphasized. "We'll have the horses to tend."

"Do it," Jake urged. "Maizy can outrun any man alive. I'll circle 'round and join you short of the creek."

"It's a good plan," Tommy said, sighing. "Better with a dozen more men."

"It'll have to do," Colonel Duncan declared. "Now let's get some rest and wait for dusk."

Sundown came soon enough. Jake could hear the Comanches laughing and carrying on across the hill, and he imagined they were celebrating the death they had dealt to the Raymonds. Tommy Carmichael, who understood a word here and there, took out a knife and clawed the ground.

"It's time," he finally told Jake.

"Keep your head down, partner," Lute urged.

Jake nodded, swallowed hard, and led Maizy through the trees that crowded the crest of the hill. He tied her a stone's throw from the Comanche camp and took a deep breath. Then, crawling on hands and knees, he crept toward the nearest tipi.

The Comanches were preoccupied with eating, and no one seemed to notice the shadowy form slipping up on their camp. Only when Jake reached the first of the lodges did he draw out his flint. He struck it with the hard iron handle of a skinning knife, and sparks sprinkled the ground. A second and a third time he struck the flint. The sound drew a surprised look from one of the younger Comanches, but he didn't locate it at first. Only when the tall grass caught fire did anyone sniff out the trouble.

"Yahyyy!" the Comanche boy exclaimed as Jake scrambled to his feet and raced toward his waiting mare.

The Comanches tossed their food aside and hurried to grab bows and rifles. Now the fire was devouring the first tipi and racing along toward the others. In dismay, the Comanches split up to battle the flames or pursue their attacker.

Jake looked back only once. There wasn't time afterward. He untied the reins from a low cedar branch and leaped up on Maizy's back. As a pair of howling boys raced blindly through the trees, Jake kicked his horse into a gallop and raced off toward the safety of the far hillside.

Other shouts soon rose as well. Jake knew his comrades were busy, too. The sound of stampeding horses mixed with curses and taunts. Jake couldn't help grinning with satisfaction as he imagined the enraged Indians discovering they had been outwitted by a handful of white men.

Meanwhile, he descended the hill and swung south and east toward the path his friends would take in making their escape from the enemy. There wasn't much light, and he soon had to slow Maizy to a trot. Before long he heard the thunderous pounding of mustang hooves, and he noticed an eerie cloud of dust choking the creek just ahead.

"Colonel!" Jake called.

"It's Jake," Lute declared as he swung over to ride alongside. "We did it, didn't we?"

"Sure did," Jake agreed, relieved to rejoin the little band.

"Did you see what you did?" Tommy asked when he swung around and joined the youngsters.

"No," Jake admitted. "I was mainly concerned with getting out of there."

"That was smart, all right," Tommy agreed. "That fire you set tore right across the hill and burned everything. I'll bet those Comanches will be lucky if they got their moccasins out before the fire ate 'em."

"That bunch won't fare too well," Lute agreed. "No, sir. We got their ponies, and all they could do was stand there throwing rocks. Didn't even have time to get armed.

"We were lucky," Tommy judged. "And we could still hear from those fellows. I've known Comanches to walk twenty, thirty miles in one night when they weren't chasing half as good a batch of horses."

The notion soured Jake, and he hoped the colonel would decide to return to Collin County soon. Instead, as they drove the captured horses into the work corral, Duncan suggested working the rough edges off the Indian ponies and taking them into town with the others.

"Colonel, those Comanches know this camp," Tommy complained. "They're not more'n ten miles away. No more'n an easy walk. Mad as they are, we're sure to have visitors. Let's get on along. We can work the horses at the station."

"We'll lose a third of them getting there," Duncan argued.

"But not a third of us," Tommy observed.

"You worry too much," the colonel grumbled. "They won't come back. They've been shaken considerably. They'll be afraid."

"Can't the whole batch be blind, Colonel," Tommy insisted. "One of 'em's bound to've counted heads. The four of us won't scare anybody off."

John Duncan wasn't going to be hurried, though. Where before he might have raced to town for protection, he now was willing to take on a whole band of vengeful Comanches.

"I suppose you can't blame him," Lute said when he spread his blankets out beside Jake later that night. "He isn't seeing horses, after all. No, those are twenty-dollar gold pieces dancing on hooves."

"We couldn't get anywhere tonight," Jake noted. "To begin with, we're too tired. We don't any of us know the trail, either, and how could we hope to keep all those ponies with us?"

"Likely you're right as rain about that," Tommy said as he sat beside the fire, cradling his rifle. "But I'll bet we all of us will wish we'd kept going when morning finds us sitting here with another war on our hands."

"You really think they'll come after us?" Jake asked.

"We chased them, didn't we? They've got numbers on their side, and they know the country. What'd stop 'em?"

• • •

Jake slept fitfully that night. Tyler Raymond's ghost prowled his dreams, moaning as he drifted along on a cloud. A dozen times painted Comanches fell on the mustangers' camp, butchering everyone. Jake felt the bite of their war axes and knives. His chest filled with arrows. Twice he awoke in a cold sweat, gasping for breath. It was little satisfaction to see Lute tossing and turning as well.

When dawn broke across Mustang Flats, Colonel Duncan was already prowling the camp, rifle in hand. Tommy Carmichael was dozing nearby, but his rifle remained at hand. Only Casper seemed at ease. He was slicing strips of bacon and dropping them in a skillet.

"Well, looks like you ain't been scalped yet, boys," he called when Jake blinked his eyes and sat up.

"Feel like I've been beat on some, though," Lute grumbled as he rolled out of his blankets. "Must've found every rock in creation to put under me last night!"

"Rise and shine!" the colonel called. "Best to pack up your gear and get ready to head out."

"Sir?" Jake asked.

"I thought we were going to work the horses some more," Lute said as he pulled on his trousers.

"Colonel and I did some talking on that," Casper explained. "And then there's our friends over yonder."

Casper pointed to the far side of the creek.

Three Comanche boys sat there in plain view, watching the mustang camp.

"Got to give those Indians credit for gumption," Lute declared. "A Sharps rifle could drop 'em easy from here."

"Maybe I'll have a try at 'em," Tommy said, shaking off the morning chill.

"No point riling 'em," Casper argued. "But I'd guess by midday they'll have company. Be best not to be around when the whole batch arrives."

"I'm surprised they didn't make a try for the ponies last night," Tommy said, shaking his head.

"They did," Casper said, frowning. "Two of 'em did, anyway. Likely those other three are waiting on 'em right now. Won't be coming, though."

"Colonel Duncan?" Lute asked.

"We each of us got one," Casper boasted. "Colonel's not one to sleep easy when trouble's near."

"I didn't hear any shots," Jake said, rising nervously and gazing around.

"Knives don't make much noise," Casper explained. "Sorry to say we didn't give 'em much chance to shout. Last night I judged 'em older. Seeing their faces this morning, it's clear they weren't much older'n Tyler. Well, he's got age mates on yon hill now."

"You buried them?" Lute asked.

"Didn't think the sight of 'em would stand us in much favor with their friends," Casper said, frowning. "Now pack up your things like the colonel told you. Then grab a biscuit out of the Dutch oven and help yourself to some bacon. Once we mount up, we won't be eating again till we reach Duncan's Station."

"Figure the Comanches will follow us?" Jake asked Tommy.

"They won't get far afoot," Tommy noted. "No, if we move quick enough, we'll get off easy. It's not so far, after all."

"They wouldn't chase us to the station, would they?" Lute asked.

"No, I'd say once they see we're moving on, they'll help themselves to fresh mounts from the herds hereabouts."

Jake brightened a bit at that suggestion, and he hurried to roll up his blankets and ready Maizy for the homeward ride. Lute wasn't more than a step behind. Once breakfast was finished and the plates scraped clean, Colonel Duncan inspected the supply wagon and turned it over to Tommy Carmichael.

"You get along south fast as you can," the colonel instructed. "Casper will lead the ponies out, and you two boys will ride the flanks. I'll be up front, and Casper will bring up the rear."

"How many you figure we'll get south?" Casper asked.

"Enough," Duncan replied, gazing warily at the Comanche boys across the creek. "I believe we've dug enough graves."

"More'n enough," Casper agreed.

Tommy climbed up on the wagon and whipped the team into motion. The colonel then led his three companions toward the corral. It was time to go to work.

11

As he rode south along the flank of the herd, Jake never managed to relax. When he wasn't cutting off the escape of some pony, he was casting a wary eye at the surrounding hills for signs of pursuing Comanches. All in all, hunting mustangs had turned from a great adventure into another disappointment. Only now did he begin to realize how close to death's dark shadow he'd stepped. If he'd slipped while running from the Comanche camp, or if Maizy had stumbled, the Comanches would surely have cut him to pieces as unmercifully as they had butchered Ed Raymond.

The solitude of those long hours riding alone tore at him like eagle's talons. Every inch of his body was painted with dust, and he had to swing a bit wider than was prudent from time to time or choke from it. There was no Lute to chase away the gloom with one of his addled harmonica tunes, and no little brother's pranks to distract him. Even the wildflowers coloring the hillsides failed to break the monotony of that ride.

"Keep at it, boys!" Colonel Duncan urged as he rode a circuit around the herd. "It's best to keep 'em moving. We'll never be able to keep control if we stop shy of a corral."

It was true enough, but that didn't ease the work or lessen Jake's exhaustion.

"Wish I'd gotten some sleep last night," he

grumbled as he slumped forward onto Maizy's neck. "Watch the ponies, girl. My eyes are dying."

The mustangers managed to keep the herd together the first ten miles, but afterward the Comanche ponies in particular managed to break away in twos and threes. There was no helping it. Once a few got away, others followed. By the time Jake glimpsed the corral at Duncan Station, he counted less than twenty horses remaining in the herd.

"A poor showing," the colonel declared as he swung open the corral gate. Casper guided the horses inside, and Duncan closed the gate.

"If we get a decent price, we'll have made out all right," Casper argued.

"Better'n the Raymonds, anyhow," Lute noted. "I believe I'd rather settle for ten and have Ed and Ty along."

"Can't take those two to heart," Tommy advised. "It's hard country out here. Why, most outfits lose a man or two to snakebite or fever."

"Sure," Lute agreed sighing. "I was only thinking how it could've been me."

"Could've been all of us," Tommy insisted. "We're fortunate it wasn't. God was watching over us 'cause that was one foolish thing, chasing after those ponies! Taking 'em right from under a pack of Comanches' noses! Now there's a story to share with my grandkids. If I live long enough to have any."

Jake was too weary to take in any of the talk that followed. Nathaniel and Jefferson raced out to greet the colonel, and Duncan turned the saddle horses over to their able care.

"Kind of a poor showing, Pa," Miranda announced when she finally stepped outside.

"Could have been worse," Duncan declared. "We got some rooms for the boys? They've had a long day of it."

She eyed the dusty figures with disdain and folded her arms.

"There's plenty of room in the loft to spread your blankets," she answered. "Later, when you've had a wash, you can share the corner room."

"Barn's fine by me," Casper muttered as he turned away.

"Ready the bathwater," Colonel Duncan instructed. "I need a hot soak."

"I need my rest more," Tommy said, leaning on a fence post. "Might be I'll take you up on that hot bath tomorrow."

"Jake?" Miranda asked, lifting his chin.

"I'm used to the loft," he said, forcing a grin onto his face. "Anyhow, I couldn't sleep without Lute's snoring. I've grown accustomed to it."

"I'd take a bath, Miss Miranda," Lute said, bowing to her. "Only you ain't got enough water to get all the dust off me. Best I dump myself in the creek tomorrow."

"Might be a good idea at that," Miranda observed. "'Take that stubble-chinned fool next to you along. I hardly recognize him."

"Good to see you, too, Miranda," Jake said, laughing. He then turned and stumbled toward the barn. He followed Lute up into the loft and collapsed in the hay. He didn't bother with his blankets. He didn't even pry his boots from his swollen feet. He merely collapsed and let fatigue overwhelm him.

Jake didn't awake until midmorning. It was only the noise of Nathaniel and Jefferson coaxing the relief team out of the barn that disturbed him even then. To his surprise, Jake saw the loft was deserted. Someone had thrown a blanket over him, too, and his boots stood off to one side.

"You finally up, Jake Wetherby?" Jefferson called when Jake leaned over the rail and peered down into the barn.

"Was a little weary, Jefferson," Jake explained as he rubbed the sleep out of his eyes.

"Suppose you were," Nathaniel said, laughing. "Didn't even notice Miss Miranda pulling your boots off. Lucky you weren't peeled naked, I'd guess."

Jefferson whispered something to his companion, and the stable boys laughed loudly.

"Too late to get some breakfast?" Jake asked.

"You wash up some, I'd bet you can talk Miss Miranda out of something," Nathaniel declared. "Hurry yourself, though. Colonel's already stomping 'round, anxious to get after those horses you brought in."

"Sure," Jake grumbled. "He's never been known to give a body time to rest."

"Gave you most of the morning," Nathaniel argued. "Likely cut your pay for it, but he let you be."

114

Jake couldn't help sharing the tall black man's amusement. Moreover, Nathaniel was mostly right about wasting the morning. Jake pulled on his boots and descended the splintery ladder. In no time he'd stepped to the pump, drowned his face in cool well water, and scrubbed the dust from his hands and arms. He still wasn't fit company for a barn owl, but he hoped maybe Miranda would allow him something to eat, even if he had to share Casper's exile.

"You look some better," she said when Jake appeared at the door.

"Figure you could manage some eggs for me?" he asked. "A slice of bacon."

"Got something better," she said, ushering him inside.

Lute and Tommy shared a corner table, and Colonel Duncan sipped coffee from a mug while talking to three stage passengers. Miranda led Jake to an unoccupied table nearer the bar and hurried off to the kitchen. She returned a few minutes later with a platter of steak, a mountain of eggs, fried potatoes, and three steaming biscuits.

"Pa told me how you fought off those Indians," she whispered as she sat across the table from him. "Wasn't the smartest thing I ever heard, but I judge you earned a full belly for it."

"Thanks," he said, smiling wearily. "You know me. I don't always think things through like I should."

"Was a brave thing, sneaking up on those tipis and setting them afire. Jake, it wouldn't hurt you to be more careful. Your brothers have come by every few days to see if I had word. You'd be missed if something had happened."

"I know," he agreed. "We've buried three brothers, you know. Littler ones. They look all right, Miranda?"

"Taking on color," she observed. "Some pounds, too. The littlest one, Joshua, seemed too sad, but the other two are filling out, getting taller."

"It's good to hear."

"Guess you missed them, too."

"Well, I'm ashamed to say I didn't think much about them," Jake confessed. "Was too busy, I suppose."

"It's probably best you can put all that past you," she declared, sitting back in her chair while he gobbled a mouthful of eggs. "I think they probably miss you too much. Frank Selwyn's a good man, and Rebecca will see they get a ma's attention."

"It's my job they're doing, though," Jake muttered. "Ought to feel a little guilty about it."

"Don't," she argued. "A farmer's always glad to get three new hands come planting time."

"It's no bargain," Jake insisted. "You haven't seen those boys eat. Selwyn's going to need thirty acres of corn just to break even."

"I haven't heard him complaining any," she insisted. "Now get to eating. Pa's sure to put you to work before long."

"Yeah, I suppose so," he agreed, touching her hand lightly. "Thanks for the blanket, Miranda."

"They told you?" she asked, glaring at the corner table.

"Jefferson," Jake explained. "I suppose a woman needs to get in a little mothering practice."

"Now what does that mean?" she barked. "You figure I'm old enough to be your mother, Jake Wetherby!"

"No, but I expect you will be a ma one of these days. Don't you think?"

"Not with dusty-faced, mange-infested scoundrels like you to choose a husband from," she grumbled.

"That young preacher's unattached," Jake whispered.

"Darnell Middleton?" she exclaimed. "Jake, I've known men got shot for threatening a woman!"

He laughed a moment, then began slicing the steak into chunks suitable for chewing. She walked off to check on the needs of the stage passengers and left him to finish the breakfast alone.

Jake found mealtimes the sole respite from long hours of sweating over the ponies at the corral. Mostly he exercised Demon and the fresh-broken mustangs. Their brief run in the open had turned them rebellious, and more often than not Jake found himself bouncing off the corral rails or spitting out dust on the rocky ground.

Casper took charge of the Comanche ponies. They responded to him amazingly well. Colonel Duncan observed each pony's progress, and when a horse was deemed saddlebroken, Tommy heated up a fire, and Casper slapped a Bar JD brand on them.

Generally Casper allowed another week before he tried to shoe their hooves.

"You've done passable well with that stallion," Casper declared after Jake managed to stay atop Demon for three entire circuits around the corral. "Trick's to get him calmed down enough to take anybody on his back."

"Anybody?" Jake asked.

"We won't manage much of a price for him if he throws a rider into a pile of horse dung," Casper explained. "If he'll settle down, we can sell him for a fine piece of change."

"And if not?"

"Well, we can cut him," Casper said, frowning. "Me, I'd hate to do it. You give up half the price, and a mustang like that ought to pass his blood on."

"I've never been too high on geldings myself," Jake grumbled.

"Oh, it's the only way with some ponies," Casper argued. "A lot of men don't want just any old colt mixing with their mares. I wouldn't mind matching that Demon with one, though. Get a fine colt off him, I'd wager."

"You ever done much breeding, Casper?" Jake asked.

"Always figured if I could save enough silver to buy a little place of my own, I'd raise horses. I know 'em well enough, and you can always find a market for good ranch ponies. I don't like to think on it too much, me getting old like I am, but it's a fair dream for a youngster like you."

"How much money would it take, Casper? Couple of hundred dollars?"

"More like a thousand for a good piece of land. It takes acres to run horses. Help, too. You could always collect mustangs for a start, but you'd have to pay top dollar for a stud to get folks' attention. That's what I aim to do, anyhow."

"A thousand, huh?" Jake asked. "I'll be a lifetime managing that much money."

"Well, I've never come by as much myself," Casper admitted. "Still, it costs nothing to dream."

Jake grinned his agreement and nudged Demon into a fourth turn around the corral.

"You heard Casper, didn't you, boy?" Jake whispered. "If it was me, I'd get awful gentle. You wouldn't take to the other choice."

The stallion shook its head as if to agree, and Jake urged him into a trot.

"You're the best of the lot, Demon," Jake boasted. And to prove it, he slipped the horse out of the corral and raced up and down the Preston road.

"He's a racer, all right," Lute agreed as he helped Jake remove the saddle. "Figure I can have a try at him tomorrow?"

"If you don't mind a little battering," Jake said, grinning.

"Hope you're not taking this horse too much to heart, Jake," Lute added. "You know these ponies are sure to be sold when the market's held in McKinney. Third Monday in April."

"I might just go and buy Demon myself," Jake declared, scratching the mustang's nose. "Pair him off with Maizy and breed some colts."

"You figure the colonel to go along?"

"If I can match top bid," Jake said, pondering it. "My share from the others ought to give me enough."

"You might be giving the colonel a few points toward generosity," Lute warned. "I've known him a bit longer. Don't count on much pay from this adventure, Jake. He'll subtract what the supplies and such've cost, and split half of what's left among the crew."

"There's just what, four of us?"

"Just 'cause the Raymonds got killed and those other two rode off, it don't mean the colonel won't split our money eight ways anyhow."

"But—"

"Don't get your hopes up too high, Jake," Lute warned. "Could be he's got a better nature to him. Hell, he took you and me along, and we're neither of us half the use Casper is. If we'd kept the whole batch, he'd be in a better mind, too. But he'll have to give away some of those ponies."

"I did a man's work out there," Jake insisted, "and I'm due a fair split. Colonel Duncan's always dealt square, and I won't believe he's changed all of a sudden."

"Well, you hang on to your dreams, Jake," Lute muttered. "Me, I've seen him pinch a silver dollar till it screamed."

Jake laughed. Then, easing the bridle off Demon's nose, he let the stallion return to the other horses.

12

April greeted Texas with a series of spring showers that soon turned tempestuous. Thunder shook the land, and lightning tore the heavens. Jake alternately huddled with Lute under the eaves of the barn and stood by the corral, guarding the gate and trying to reassure the horses. The creeks surged past their banks, and some mornings Colonel Duncan led his little band of mustangers down to the crossings to pull a stagecoach out of the mud.

"Not much adventure to be found these days," Lute grumbled.

"No, but you never bad-mouth rain in Texas," Jake insisted. "Not when you recall how it gets come August."

As the day of the McKinney market approached, Jake managed to draw John Duncan aside.

"Colonel, I was wondering," Jake began.

"Wondering what?" Duncan asked.

"About Demon," Jake explained. "You know he's settled down considerable, and—"

"Turned into a fine animal," the colonel agreed. "I'd judge him the best of the bunch at this point."

"I've got awful close to him, Colonel. You know he tossed the Comanche who was trying to steal him. Maizy's not so young anymore, and—"

"You'd like me to make a present of him to

you, huh?" Duncan asked, frowning. "Jacob Henry, I signed you on to do a man's work, not to—"

"Haven't I done it?" Jake asked. "Everything you expected? More besides, even?"

"I'd say so," the colonel confessed. "You have to understand I didn't ride out to Mustang Flats for the amusement of fighting Comanches or chewing trail dust. It was to turn a profit."

"I know that."

"If I give each man a pony, I won't have more than a dozen left to sell. You wouldn't deem it right to give you a horse and not allow Casper one? Lute? Tom?"

"No, sir," Jake agreed. "I wasn't expecting any gift. Colonel, I don't take anything I don't earn. You know that."

"But you still expect me to turn Demon over to you?"

"I figured you could consider him my share of the sale."

"Oh?" Duncan asked, laughing. "Son, just what measure of pay are you expecting?"

"Well, we all agreed you would take half. We four should split the rest."

"I believe we agreed you would have an eighth, Jake. Wasn't that it?"

"You won't be paying Sturgess or McCullough," Jake noted. "Nor the Raymonds."

"I settled with the Raymonds before we left," Duncan explained. "Paid off a debt they owed. Truth is, I'll lose on that bargain."

"And the others?"

"I thought to double Casper's portion and apply the rest against the extra expenses we've had. This excursion cost much more than I anticipated."

"I don't fault Casper drawing double pay," Jake said, sighing. "But I've done more than an eighth of the work, Colonel. Even an eighth of twenty horses ought to equal Demon, though."

"And what about costs?"

"You've spent considerable, Colonel. I'll warrant that. But you get half the sale price—"

"Half the profit," Duncan explained. "If we manage twenty dollars a head—and that's being optimistic where some of these animals are concerned—it amounts to four hundred dollars. Taking out supplies, shoes, and equipment, I'd guess we clear a hundred twenty maybe. Your portion of sixty is—"

"Less'n ten dollars," Jake said, dropping his eyes. "Made more riding to town for you."

"We had bad luck, son," the colonel said, shaking his head. "That's all. We might have brought in a hundred head. You would have made good money then, but it would hardly have been fifty dollars. I expect to bid Demon up there at least."

"Yes, sir," Jake said, trying to hide the bitterness flooding his insides.

"You don't think I've done right by you, Jake?"

"I don't know for certain," Jake answered. "Seems a poor return for the risks I've taken, nor the effort. But I trust you to judge our agreement for what it was, and I'll abide by what you say."

"A man couldn't ask more," Duncan argued.

"Jake, I wish I could see my way clear to—"

"No, you explained it all," Jake declared. "I understand."

"You don't hold it against me, then?"

"No," Jake said, shaking the man's hand. As he turned and walked away, though, Jake recalled something his father had told him. *Life teaches you things. Swallow the bitter ones and don't make the same mistake. It's the best way to learn.*

His father had learned plenty of hard lessons, and now Jake, too, was gaining an education. When the colonel assembled them for the ride to McKinney, he and Miranda were both surprised to see Jake tying his blanket roll behind his saddle.

"Planning a trip, Jake?" Miranda asked.

"Not a long one," he explained. "Thought to visit my family."

"You'll be coming back, then," she said, calming.

"To chop wood?" Jake asked. "Colonel, you don't figure to ride back to Mustang Flats, do you?"

"Not before summer," Duncan answered. "But there's work here a man could do."

"Maybe Jake and I'll scare up a few ponies ourselves," Lute said, nodding to Jake. "We could make ten dollars shooting wolves for the bounty."

"We could do better," Duncan argued.

"We could," Lute agreed. "And some of us will, Colonel."

"Wouldn't hurt you none to cut a better deal

with those boys," Casper grumbled. "They stood real tall when it counted."

"You running this outfit, Casper?" the colonel barked.

"Nope," Casper replied. "And so long as I eat regular and don't have too many women pestering me to take baths, I don't much care about anything. I can tell when a man and a horse make a pair, though."

"Get mounted," Duncan growled. "We've got ponies to drive to town."

There was always a need for horses in Texas. Jake had heard those words a hundred times. But when Colonel John Duncan displayed his string in McKinney, he found few buyers. Cash money was never in great supply in Collin County, and a rancher from Weatherford named Spence bought ten of the mustangs for a hundred dollars.

"No way to get rich, eh, boys?" the colonel said, frowning as he accepted payment.

Colonel Duncan auctioned the others, but top price was just thirty dollars before Jake led Demon out for the bidders to eye.

"I got fifteen dollars, Jake," Lute whispered, offering the money. "Casper's offered another five, and the colonel could draw on our wages for another thirty-five."

"I couldn't take your money," Jake insisted.

"Would be an investment," Lute argued.

Jake halfway grinned. He tied Demon to a post in the center of the corral and climbed up on the rail fence with the other bidders.

"What do I hear for this fine specimen?" Duncan asked.

"Thirty dollars!" Jake shouted, gazing hard at the other bidders. Two laughed and climbed down from the fence. Another smiled in surprise.

"Thirty-five," Spence countered, drawing a roll of bank notes from his pocket.

"Forty," Jake said nervously.

"Forty-five," Spence barked.

"Fifty," Jake said, eyeing Spence pleadingly.

"Sixty," Spence bid. "And before you say another word, son, I want to see your cash. I've seen sellers seed crowds before, and I won't—"

"He's no plant," Casper said, turning to the colonel. "Can't you see the boy loves that stallion?"

"Bid's sixty," Duncan said, turning to Jake. "I'm holding thirty-five dollars wages promised against the bid. How much do you have on you, Jake?"

"Seventeen," Jake said, trembling.

"I got another ten," Casper declared.

"Sixty-two, eh?" Spence said, twirling the ends of his mustache. "I'll make my offer sixty-five, then."

Jake hung his head and held back an urge to kick something.

"Sixty-five once," Duncan called. "Twice. Sold to Homer Spence for sixty-five dollars."

"Sorry, son," Spence said, offering his hand. "I suspect I need that horse more than you do, though."

Jake turned away from the rancher and dashed off to where Maizy stood, waiting.

"Don't take it to heart, Jake," Lute urged as he rested his hand on Jake's shoulder. "I tried to warn you, but..."

"I know," Jake said, returning Lute's money. "We did all we could."

"We could always turn horse thief," Casper added as he joined the youngsters. "Weatherford's a fair piece of country west of here. That Spence fellow can't hang around here long, looking for a horse."

"Likely Demon'll throw him proper," Lute suggested. "Break a bone or two, and Spence'll sell him cheap."

But Spence had already thrown a saddle onto Demon and was mounting the stallion that very moment. At first Demon fought the big Texan, but Spence held firm control.

"You did too good a job with him," Casper observed. "Be other horses, Jake. Other years."

"Sure," Jake agreed. He still had Maizy, after all, and it was probably foolish to ever have considered keeping two horses.

"You coming back to the station, Jake?" Lute asked.

"No, I don't have the heart," Jake answered.

"Tom and I'll be driving freight for a time," Casper explained. "You'd be a welcome sight on layover days."

"I thought maybe we could find those brothers of yours and do some swimming," Lute suggested.

"I'm riding down to Harrison's Crossroads just now," Jake told them. "Pay a visit to my sister. Maybe I'll pass a couple of days with the boys down at Frank Selwyn's place. You come along, Lute, and we'll splash half the creek out of its banks."

"Maybe I'll meet you there in a day or so," Lute answered. "Colonel hasn't told me to ride just yet, and if he'll feed me, I guess I'll hang around at the station."

"I can't go back there," Jake said, dropping his chin onto his chest. "I don't suppose I was exactly cheated, but I don't feel fair-treated, either."

"Sure, we know," Casper said, slapping Jake on the back. "There's fair and there's fair. I figure when a man stands elbow to elbow with you when the Comanches are after your hair, there's more'n money in the bargain."

"Don't blame Colonel Duncan," Jake told them. "Wasn't his fault I expected more."

"Don't take out the hurt, though, eh?" Lute asked. "We'll be swimming that creek by and by, Jake. I promise you that. And maybe later chasing mustangs again."

"I wouldn't say no to that," Jake replied.

They stood for a moment, searching for something more to say, but everything necessary had been spoken. Tommy Carmichael hurried over and passed a ten-dollar gold piece into Jake's hand.

"From the colonel," Tommy explained. "He didn't figure you would take it so hard, Jake. He won't own up to it, but I suspect he's short of money himself."

"Maybe," Jake said, stuffing the gold piece in his pocket and shaking Tommy's hand.

"Watch yourself, Jake," the ex-cavalryman

advised. "If you ever need a friend in a tight spot, know there's men around that would consider it a pleasure to stand with you."

"Thanks," Jake replied.

"See you at the creek," Lute whispered as Jake mounted Maizy.

"Watch out for Comanches!" Tommy urged.

Casper waved, and Jake grinned an answer. Turning Maizy slowly, he nudged her southward, away from the market and along toward Harrison's Crossroads.

He took his time riding, for the wind was crisp that morning, and the sky bright and clear. Maizy enjoyed the easy pace, too.

"Why hurry, huh?" Jake asked her. "No place waiting on us, after all. Nobody."

When he rode up the dusty trail toward Harrison's Store, he passed Betsy, sitting in a swing on Doc Springfield's porch with his small brother Joe.

"Howdy!" Jake called.

Betsy's face betrayed a prideful smile as she returned Jake's wave.

Jane Mary trotted over from her place and stood, hands on hips, waiting for Jake to halt. He did, and she halfway pulled him out of the saddle.

"Jake, look at you!" she cried. "Grown right out of your britches! I hardly know you!"

"I haven't changed that much," he argued, slipping his toe from the left stirrup and dropping to the ground beside her. She ran her hand along the side of his face and scowled.

"Wouldn't hurt to try a razor on those whiskers," Jane Mary declared. "I'm surprised Miranda didn't insist."

"I've been pretty busy," he explained. "I guess I should have stopped at the creek and sorted myself out some, though."

"Ah, there's no one here to impress," Jane Mary said, wrapping an arm around his waist. "I've seen you worse. I'll heat up some water, and you can shave proper."

"Sure, sis," Jake agreed.

"You'll stay awhile, then?"

"If it's not too much trouble. I'm not going back to the colonel's."

"Through mustanging, huh?" Jane Mary asked. "Well, I want to hear all about it later on. I'll expect you to stay on here at least a week. Martin's in sore need of some help, and what with Betsy and the baby gone, the house feels almost empty."

"She got herself married to the doc, then?"

"Two weeks ago," Jane Mary said, frowning. "Some deem she hurried herself, but what else was there to do? No more than a girl, with a baby and all. Doc's little ones needed tending, too. I believe it's a good thing all around."

"Seen the boys lately?"

"Only yesterday. They'll be awful glad to see you. Josh never stops jabbering away about you, and Jer's counting the days till he turns sixteen and can go mustanging with you.

"He's a fool to hurry," Jake grumbled.

"It didn't turn out, did it?"

"We had our share of trouble," Jake said as he led Maizy around toward the small horse corral Martin Browning had built back of the house. As he stripped his gear from Maizy, Jake narrated the adventure at Mustang Flats. He read the pain and concern that filled his sister's eyes, and part of him wanted to hold back. The tale needed sharing, though.

"I blame myself for all that," Jane Mary said when Jake finished. "I should've insisted you come stay with us."

"You took in Betsy and the baby," Jake observed. "Besides, I needed some time to myself. It wasn't all bad, either. I met some fine friends, and I grew some."

"Hardened you," Jane Mary observed. "I'll agree it did that. Being on your own isn't all you expect, though. Those first weeks after I left home, I thought I'd choke on the loneliness. A body needs family, Jake. Solitude is the worst sort of trial."

"I haven't found much in it to recommend," Jake agreed.

"Come along inside now," Jane Mary said, taking his arm. "I'll heat water. First you can shave. Then maybe I'll get a bath ready."

"You and Ma," Jake said, laughing. "I never did know a woman so eager to see a man wash!"

"Jake, you're my brother and I love you," Jane Mary said, hugging him. "But you've spent too much time around horses. I'm afraid I'd be kind to compare your scent to a polecat. I deem it a Christian duty to return you to civilization."

131

"What's that got to do with taking a bath?" Jake asked.

"I can't very well sit down to dinner with a skunk!" she exclaimed.

"Figure you'll have to squeeze lemons to get the smell out, do you?"

"Like when Jordy happened across those stinkers last summer?" she asked, breaking into a frenzy of laughter. "Now that's the funniest thing I've ever seen, that skinny little boy racing across the barnyard, shedding his clothes and howling like a stuck pig."

"I miss those times," Jake confessed.

"So do I," she whispered. "So do I, Jake."

13

Jake passed that night and all of the next day at Harrison's Crossroads with Jane Mary and Martin. It was a warming time for all of them, but as he helped Martin mend a saddle, Jake clearly saw there wasn't enough work to keep two men employed.

"Work goes faster with company around," Martin insisted. "And I can always make boots and saddlebags. There's a handsome profit to be made selling both in Dallas."

"I never have been much good sewing," Jake said, frowning. "You'd wind up doing all the work, and I'd go crazy watching."

"Jace Harrison might could use some help,"

Martin suggested. "And a man can always fell trees and sell the wood."

"Only if it's off his wood lot," Jake argued. "Don't worry about me, Marty. I'll find something that needs doing."

"You might talk with the colonel."

"Maybe later. Just now I'm still feeling a little stung."

Later, sitting with Jane Mary, he read anxiety in his sister's eyes.

"Stay," she pleaded. "The town's growing. You have a knack for building things, and there isn't a better man around for working with animals."

"I'd judge there to be several," Jake replied. "Anyhow, I thought to visit the boys on Spring Creek. No need to make plans till afterward."

"You'd be welcome to stay at the Selwyn place," Jane Mary observed. "Frank's got Silas out running in mavericks. He butchers them for the meat and works the hides. Martin, for one, buys them."

"I'll consider it," Jake promised.

"I'd like to have you nearby, Jake," she added. "For the brothers' sake. In case trouble comes along, too."

"I never saw any trouble you couldn't handle," he told her with a grin. "I wouldn't mind sticking in Collin County, but you know how Wetherbys are. We've got an itch to wander."

"I would've thought you'd scratched that itch up in Denton County," Jane Mary grumbled. "You do what you have to, but don't forget you've got family eager to have you."

"I won't," Jake pledged. "It's a comfort, too."

That next morning after breakfast, Jake saddled Maizy and rode along Spring Creek toward the Selwyn farm. Halfway there he came across his brothers on their way to the new schoolhouse located on the creek just west of town.

"Look there!" Josh shouted, dropping his slate and racing toward Jake.

"Jake!" Jericho yelled.

"Watch out there, Josh!" Jordy warned. "Like as not there's a sheriff's posse trailing him."

Josh never hesitated, though. He tore along the creek bank and climbed up onto Maizy's rump.

"We missed you," the eleven-year-old said, battering Jake's back. "Went out to Duncan's Station a dozen times to see you, but you weren't there."

"Gave up too soon," Jake said, sliding his brother around in front of him. "You've gone and grown tall, Josh!"

"You're some bigger yourself," Josh said, grinning. "Come to take us off chasing horses?"

"No," Jake said, "although the idea's tempting."

"Beats school, I'll bet," Jericho said as he walked up with Jordy.

"School's not half so bad as you think," Jake told them. "You promised Ma to finish. Besides, I near got myself scalped mustanging."

"Tell us," Josh pleaded.

"You've got school to get to," Jake declared. "I'll be around this afternoon when you get home."

"Seems to me we've been in school every day since we come to live with the Selwyns," Jericho grumbled. "I'd say we were due a day off."

"Anybody can get lost on the way," Jordy added.

"You all promised—" Jake argued.

"Don't go telling us you never got confused and missed getting to school, Jake," Jordy said, grinning. "Jer and I remember plenty of times when we went swimming or fishing instead."

"That was before I turned respectable," Jake argued.

"That what you turned?" Jericho asked, laughing. "To look at you, I'd say you've gone and become a renegade horse thief."

"No such a thing!"

"Come on, Jake," Jordy pleaded. "We get bossed enough by Miz Selwyn. She's near broken her hand whipping Si into shape! Makes Jane Mary seem sweet-natured."

"She's not hitting you?" Jake asked, the color rising in his face. "Josh?"

"No, she's kind to a fault," Josh explained.

"Truth be told," Jericho added, "Si could use a bashing now and again. Wouldn't hurt any of us, either. You get two cross words off her, we'd all likely die of shock."

"She's nice, Jake," Josh insisted. "Jordy just likes to rile folks up."

"Yeah, he does," Jake agreed. "Any excuse to dodge chores, too, eh?"

"Learned from a close relative," Jordy responded. "Don't remember who exactly, do you, Jake?"

They enjoyed a laugh at Jake's expense. Then Jordy walked over, set his slate and two books on the bank, and began peeling off his clothes. Before Jake quite knew what was happening, Jordy was splashing into the creek and urging his brothers to follow.

"School, Jordy," Josh complained.

"Jordy's right," Jericho argued. "We've had enough school for a time. Seems to me like a family reunion's called for."

With that said, Jericho climbed out of his overalls, kicked off his shoes, and splashed into the creek.

"I can't go by myself," Josh said, grinning at Jake. "They'd only have at me for Jordy and Jer missing."

"Go on then, Peanut," Jake said, helping Josh off the horse. "I guess it is too dusty to go to school today. A bath never hurt anybody, after all."

"Then get along in!" Jordy yelled.

Jake nudged Maizy along to a slight rise and dismounted. There was good grass for the mare to chew there, and he left her to graze while he undressed. By the time Josh waded out into the creek, Jake was hurrying along behind him.

The brothers were hours in that creek, swimming and splashing and wrestling. The water had a chill bite to it, but Jake found the company more than compensated for it. He hadn't had an all-out honest-to-God good time in ages, and he guessed his brothers hadn't had one, either, to see them hopping around, yelling and tossing mud at one another.

It wasn't until later, when they lay on the bank, drying themselves as they shared the lunch Rebecca Selwyn had packed, that Jake spoke of Mustang Flats. The boys sat spellbound while he told of running down the mustangs. Their faces grew long and their breathing near stopped when Jake described Tyler Raymond's dying.

"Not much older'n me, huh?" Josh whispered.

"Older than Jeremiah," Jericho said, frowning. "That's how dying is out here, I guess. Quick. Early sometimes."

"Makes you mindful how sweet life is," Jake told his brothers. "You know, when I was out there riding along, alone, I couldn't help remembering how I used to hate sharing that fool room with all three of you. Now I miss those days something awful. You don't know how good you have it, I guess."

"You still miss Ma and Pa, Jake?" Josh asked.

"Just every day," Jake answered. "Every single day."

"Yeah," Jericho agreed. "Maybe not so bad as I used to, but bad enough."

"You figure we'll ever get all back together, Jake?" Jordy asked, losing his grin. "Maybe have our own place?"

"I think about it sometimes," Jake confessed, "but who knows what's going to happen? I mean, who would have dreamed a big man like Pa would catch cold and die?"

"You make a lot of money mustanging?" Jericho asked.

"Ten dollars," Jake said, sighing. "Not much of a start on a farm, is it?"

"I never took to farming anyway," Josh declared. "Pigs and chickens. Always pigs and chickens."

"Peanut, you're a born Wetherby," Jake declared, rubbing Josh's hair. "I'll have to teach you how to rope a wild mustang."

"I'd settle for a story," Josh said, jabbing Jake in the ribs with a halfhearted elbow.

"Then listen carefully while I tell you the hair-curling, spine-tingling story of Jacob Henry Wetherby's escape from the Comanche nation."

"What?" Jericho cried.

"Listen good," Jake urged. "It's not every day you're in the company of a genuine heroic Indian fighter."

Jake shared the tale, smiling as his brothers eyed the nearby trees for signs of prowling raiders. Jordy grinned and Jericho scowled. Josh slid a hair closer and hung on to Jake's shoulder.

"They might've killed you," he whispered when Jake finished.

"Naw," Jake said, laughing. "I'm too slippery to get caught by any Comanche."

"Ole Miz Saxon caught you stealing those peaches back home," Jericho said, shaking his head. "And I'll bet her switching isn't anything to what those Comanches would've done."

"Si's told us stories," Josh added. "All 'bout how the Comanches cut people up."

For an instant Jake remembered Ed Raymond, and his face paled.

"Yeah," Jake muttered. "Just stories, though."

No one spoke for a few minutes afterward. Then Jordy walked over to his clothes and slid a shirt over his bony shoulders.

"Time we got ourselves dressed," he declared. "Won't be long before Amy and Christy Anders'll be along."

"Best cover up, Jer," Josh said, laughing. "Wouldn't want to show your girlfriend everything!"

Jericho turned a shade of purple as he dashed over to his overalls. Jake noticed none of them wasted much time, even though he judged they were a couple of hours ahead of any returning scholars.

"What'll you do now, Jake?" Jericho asked as he pulled his boots on. "Go back to the colonel or stay hereabouts?"

"I thought maybe I'd see if I can wrangle a meal out of Miz Selwyn," Jake replied. "She invited me once upon a time."

"We were going to invite you when we went up to the station," Jordy explained. "To look at you, you could use some feeding."

"I didn't notice any extra pounds hanging on you three, either," Jake complained.

"We're downright fat pigs put up next to you, Jake," Josh declared. "Bet Miz Selwyn'll bake a pie if she knows you're coming."

"Let's hurry along and tell her," Jordy suggested. "Only don't say we didn't go to school. No point in stirring up any storms."

"No," Jake agreed. "Been enough of those lately."

• • •

That evening as he sat between Jordy and Josh at the long oak table in the Selwyns' dining room, Jake felt awkward. His brothers were dressed in their Sunday best, with white shirts and string ties. Frank Selwyn looked like an Austin banker, and his wife Rebecca wore a shiny pearl necklace. Even the little Selwyn children, six-year-old Willie, his two-year-old brother Gibson, and baby Joel, were scrubbed clean and sitting at their miniature table in the corner. Jake, in contrast, had only his ragged woolens and buckskin jacket.

"I hear from the boys you've had quite an adventure," Frank said, smiling at Jake.

"Been fightin' Indians," Si observed. "To hear tell, were what, five of you raided the whole Comanche horse herd?"

"Just four," Jordy boasted. "Jake burned their camp single-handed, though."

"Wasn't so much," Jake said, silently pleading for his brothers to be quiet. "Just a small raiding party, and we didn't manage to hold on to many of the horses."

"Shame that," Frank said, sighing. "You could have made a nice profit off it."

"Not the way horses are selling in Mc-Kinney," Jake grumbled.

"Prices are off on everything," Frank noted. "Still, it must have been a real adventure. I only saw Comanches once in my whole life, and there were just two of them."

"Two's enough," Jake declared.

"More than enough," Frank agreed. "I

hate to admit it, but there were six of us, and we weren't about to make any kind of a stand. Hightailed it away fast as our horses would carry us."

"Thank the Lord for prudence," Rebecca said, laughing. "I remember the time you boys' ma held off that crowd of savages. That's what I consider courage."

"Me, too," Jake said, sighing. "On the Indians' part. Ma was no one to tangle with. No sir!"

They all laughed at the notion. Then Rebecca bowed her head, and the others followed suit.

"Joshua?" she asked.

"Yes'm," Josh said, swallowing. He then spoke the words of a short prayer his mother had taught him two summers before. Jake felt the words cut their way deep into his heart, and he nodded at Josh with approval afterward.

"That's a fine sentiment," Rebecca declared.

"Was one of Ma's favorites," Josh said, smiling. "I thought Jake'd like it."

"We're all grateful to have him with us," she said, "I hope you'll stay the night. The boys will certainly want to hear more about your adventures. There's scarcely been time for much of a visit, what with them getting out of school so late."

Jordy glanced away, and Jericho coughed. Josh stared at his plate in guilty silence.

"Oh, I see," she said, shaking her head. "Should've known."

"I'm afraid it's my fault," Jake told her. "We haven't seen much of each other, and—"

"Boys never need half an excuse for neglecting their lessons on a sunny day," Rebecca insisted. "They've been too good by far since coming to live with us. I'm almost relieved to find out they finally fell off the wagon, so to speak."

"I never went to school more'n three days a week," Si confessed between mouthfuls of roast beef. "Of course, I'm no great shakes of a reader, either. I can build fences and patch roofs, though."

"And spin tall tales," Jericho observed. "Don't forget what you do best, Si."

They laughed a bit, and Si grinned broadly.

"Everybody should have a trade," Si agreed.

"Sure, but I do wish you were faster with a hammer, nephew," Frank said. "This spring's been hard on fences, and last week the wind tore half the shingles off your pa's old barn, Jake."

"I helped build that barn," Jake said, sighing.

"Seems to me you'd be the perfect man to patch it, then," Rebecca observed. "I'd guess the house could do with some fixing up, too."

"We could use your help, all right," Frank agreed. "If you haven't got anything hurrying you on, that is. Wouldn't hold you from it."

"The boys would surely enjoy a longer visit," Rebecca argued. "Wouldn't you?"

Jericho, Jordy, and Josh all howled their answer, and little Willie even managed a high-pitched "Yes!"

"I might not be able to pay you cash, understand," Frank explained, "but maybe you'd take it in trade. Rebecca always has a spare bolt of fabric set by. She could make you up some shirts, maybe some trousers from that brown wool."

"I do appear a hair threadbare," Jake admitted. "I'd consider it generous of you."

"Then you're no businessman," Frank said, shaking his head. "I'm grateful all the same."

"No, it's me's grateful for all the looking after you've given my brothers," Jake told them. "I wanted 'em with me, you know, but I was wrong not to see they're better off here."

"Well, for a while we'll all of us be together," Rebecca said, smiling warmly at Jake. "That's bound to be best of all."

14

Jake passed the night in a corner room with his brothers, Si Garrett, and little Willie Selwyn, sleeping on a straw mattress near the ash slat bed Josh and Jordy shared. The straw wasn't soft, nor was the hard floor enticing like the feather bed at Jane Mary's, but he found the rustling of his brothers and the heavier breathing of Jericho and Si a balm. Jake wasn't used to silence, and he awoke rarely refreshed to the sound of a cock that next morning.

"Morning, Jake," Josh called as he rolled

off his bed and scrambled into a pair of over-alls.

"Hogs and chickens?" Jake asked, grinning.

"Nope," Josh replied with a laugh. "Milking."

"Willie gets to feed the chickens," Jericho explained as he roused Jordy. "I get hog duty."

"Everybody works on a farm," Josh observed. "What'll you do, Jake?"

"Help me load shingles onto a wagon," Si suggested, yawning. "Best we turn to it, too, 'fore Brother Frank goes and figures out somethin' else to tack on."

"Well, unlike some folks, I've never been afraid of work," Jake boasted.

"Then you come to the right place," Si grumbled. "There's never any end to it here-abouts."

"Well," Jake told the sixteen-year-old, "you might have continued your schooling."

"He reads fine, and his penmanship's past help," Jericho observed. "Miz Hayes wasn't about to tolerate his pranks. She sent him packing."

"I never much took to books," Si con-fessed. "Give me a huntin' gun and a camp-fire anytime."

"Can't shingle a roof with either one," Jake observed.

"No, but a man can't hammer all the day," Si argued. "I expect us to find a moment or two of distraction."

"See?" Jericho asked Jake. "He's pretty hopeless. Watch out he doesn't lead you astray."

"Lead Jake astray?" Jordy asked, laughing. "More apt to be t'other way 'round."

Jake gave Jordy a halfhearted elbow and hurried out the door. Si wasn't long in following, and the two of them trotted to the barn and piled bundles of ash shingles in the back of the old Wetherby wagon.

"Will that be enough?" Jake asked, gazing at the four stacks. "Pa and I split four or five times that many."

"I don't mean to strip the whole roof off," Si grumbled. "It's just a barn, after all. You don't have to tar-paper it like a house."

"We did."

"Then I'll get some paper to patch those places. Jake, you'll end up making this a job of work."

"I've gone and reformed my wayward days, Si."

"Fine thing to tell me now."

Jake laughed and looked on while Si rummaged around in the tack room. Shortly he appeared with several sheets of tar paper.

"You don't mind if we get some breakfast before headin' out, do you?" Si asked.

"Not if your aunt cooks eggs like she prepares roast beef," Jake answered. "I can always eat."

"Come on," Si grumbled, waving Jake along.

They took their places at the big table and waited for Rebecca to bring platters. Jake reached for a plate of eggs, but Jordy restrained him.

"Jordan, I believe it's your turn to bless the

food," Rebecca said, and Jordy emitted a subtle moan.

"Thanks, Lord, for your bounty," Jordy said, managing a solemn tone with considerable difficulty. "Watch over us, and help us not to stray too far from the path. Thanks, too, for leading Jake here to share this time with us. Amen."

Jake and his brothers added another "amen." He noticed Rebecca Selwyn grinning, and Si had a hard time stifling a laugh.

"I especially liked that remark about straying from the path," Frank said, grinning. "You'll remember it as you head for school, won't you, boys?"

"Yes, sir," Josh replied. Jericho and Jordy nodded their agreement.

Afterward, mouths were too full of ham, eggs, and potatoes to converse. The sun was rising, and work was waiting, after all. When Rebecca dismissed them from breakfast, Jake barely had a moment to bid his brothers a farewell. They grabbed their slates, books, and lunch sacks as they headed out the door.

"We'll have us a swim when we get back, Jake," Josh hollered.

"Sure," Jordy added. "Maybe we'll shoot ourselves a deer, too."

Jake waved them on their way and followed Si to the waiting wagon. Together they hitched a pair of mules to the wagon and started west toward what had once been the Wetherby place.

It troubled Jake some, rumbling along that familiar ground, feeling the bounce of the wagon as he had so many times before. Tall grass had invaded the garden plots his mother had so carefully tilled. The coops and pens were deserted, and the buildings had fallen into disrepair. The windows of the house were so clouded with dust, Jake didn't even notice the curtains had been removed.

"Barn's the trouble spot," Si said, pointing to bare patches where wind and hail had stripped away shingles. Remnants of tar paper waved in the breeze like eerie black fingers.

"I'll fetch a ladder," Jake said, climbing down even before Si had the wagon stopped.

"Back of the coop," Si called.

"Wouldn't I know that?" Jake asked. "I used to rest it there."

"Didn't know," Si said, shrugging his shoulders as he halted the wagon and set its brake. "Have a good stretch, Jake, and let's have a look."

"I've seen enough," Jake muttered. "Let's get to work."

Si shook his head and spat. Jake laughed a reply.

"Nothin' to spoil a mornin' like an eager partner," Si declared.

"Unless it's a thunderstorm," Jake observed, pointing to a line of black clouds forming on the northern horizon.

"Ain't we had enough rain?" Si asked, gazing skyward.

"Come on," Jake urged, setting the ladder against the side of the barn and starting his climb. "Let's see if we can't beat the rain for once."

Si joined Jake on the roof and began stripping away warped and useless shingles with a claw hammer while Jake cut away the tattered sections of tar paper. The beams below remained sound, and it was really only a matter of patching spots here and there. Although Si grumbled considerably about the pace, Jake managed to tack squares of tar paper across all the gaps by midday. He then turned to help with the shingles.

"I remember how Pa and I put the first roof on," Jake said as he grabbed a handful of ash slices. "It was July, and the sun close to baked us."

"Not much sun today," Si muttered.

"Not raining yet, though," Jake observed.

"Don't you figure to stop and eat?"

"Might start up raining any minute," Jake said, frowning. "We can work a little longer before we die of starvation, don't you suppose?"

Just then Si hammered a shingle over the loft. To his surprise, a large bird fluttered up through the hole, flapping its wings a moment before diving back inside.

"Holy hell!" Si exclaimed, crab-walking his way to the ladder and hurrying off the roof.

"What's the matter with you?" Jake asked, laughing. "Haven't you ever seen a barn owl before?"

"Sure, and I know it's no end of bad luck!" Si shouted. "Now, let me think. There's a remedy. Walk backward twice around the barn. Come on, Jake. You saw it, too. You got to join in the cure."

"Si?" Jake cried. "I'm in the middle of nailing these shingles."

"You don't come down, lightnin's goin' to strike this barn and fry your hide. I know about such things. Don't forget how I warned you about the omens before your ma died."

"All right," Jake said, sighing as he abandoned the work and climbed down the ladder. There was no arguing with Si about omens and charms. He was more superstitious than any other boy in creation.

Jake felt like a fool, walking backward around the barn, but Si seemed genuinely relieved when they finished.

"No point in reshinglin' a roof that'll burn down," Si declared. "Now, long as we're down here, we might as well chew some biscuits and beef. Becky made plenty, and she threw in slices of cold peach pie special."

"I guess it is past noon," Jake admitted. "I'll fetch us some water from the well."

Jake hadn't much more than filled a bucket and returned to the wagon before the earth shook.

"Thunder," Si noted.

"Sure you remembered the right remedy?" Jake asked, laughing as he stuffed slices of dry roast beef between two halves of a biscuit.

"Maybe it was three," Si confessed. His eyes betrayed concern, and when a streak of fire raced down from the sky and splintered a willow down at the creek, he jumped a foot in the air. The mules screamed and raced off, spilling Jake and the shingles out of the wagon bed.

"Lord!" Jake said, picking himself up off the ground.

"Best we get along inside," Si urged, waving toward the house. Jake followed somewhat reluctantly. It wasn't raining yet, and they were only an hour or so from finishing the roof. A second thunderclap spurred him along, though, and a third boomed down the creek, rattling every window in the house.

"Three turns!" Si said, kicking the door to the main room. "Three, stupid!"

Lightning tore at the heavens, but the resulting sounds were farther off. Then a terrific roar knocked Jake off his feet. His ears stung and his head pounded. Across the way flames licked at the side of the barn.

"Three times!" Si screamed.

Jake shook off a growing dizziness and staggered to his feet. Gazing around at the dust-covered dog-run cabin, he sighed. Once not so long ago that place had been full of life. As the barn exploded in dark gray smoke and amber flame, he realized it was another reminder of the life that had slipped away from him.

"Lord, Jake, where's the rain?" Si asked. "Dry as the prairie grass is, it best start rainin' soon."

"The wind's blowing," Jake observed. "Si, if the grass catches fire, it'll sweep right down the creek and burn everything between here and town."

"Frank's place," Si mumbled.

"The school," Jake added. "Come on. We've got work to do."

Jake gazed but a moment at the barnyard. A rutted trail separated the buildings from the grass-covered prairie beyond. If the wind remained constant, it would provide an adequate firebreak.

"Got to stop it up yonder," Si observed, pointing to the thick grass to the east.

"Start a backfire," Jake agreed. "It isn't crossing the creek. We can cut it off at the bend if we get a little help from the wind."

"Or if it'd rain some," Si added.

Jake hurried toward the barn, tore a plank from the wall, and raced on toward the creek. He gave a hundred yards of grass to the fire and started scraping the prairie beyond. It was a simple enough plan—clear a path and set the adjacent grass afire. When the firestorm from the west closed in, it would suck the backfire toward it, burning the grass in between. Without fuel, the fire would starve.

The wind was tricky, though, and there was a lot of ground to clear. Jake hoped and prayed the fire would take some time devouring the barn and give them a chance.

"Hurry!" Jake urged as he dragged his plank along the rocky ground, tearing grass up by the roots with the jagged nails protruding from the board. Si had a second board now and was following along, widening the little trench. Already smoke was curling up from the prairie, though.

Jake managed to get a narrow line finished before the barn collapsed, but he knew he was facing long odds once the walls fell and the full force of the wind drove the fire across the prairie.

"Lord, help us," Si muttered.

"Wet your shirt," Jake said as he tore his own off and raced to the creek. With the wet rag ready, Jake pulled out his flints and sent sparks flying into the yellow grass. Instantly, blades of buffalo grass glowed yellow, and soon flames rose. Whenever they threatened to cross the little trench, Jake beat them out with his shirt. Soon a charred wall three yards wide blunted the fire alongside the creek.

Si had less luck with his section. The fire leaped across the trench in three places, and in spite of every effort, it raged onward.

"Jake, we got to get out of here!" Si shouted as Jake plunged ever nearer the fire, beating at flames and stomping at singed grass.

"We have to halt it here!" Jake insisted. "Once the wind gets up, it'll eat half the county. Frank's crops! Our orchard."

Si hurried back to the creek to wet his shirt a second time while Jake struggled on. Already his arms were black and the legs of his trousers were tattered. The hairs on his shins were burned away in eerie patterns, and he found himself laughing.

"You won't beat me, fire!" Jake shouted. "Come on, rain! Turn it back, wind!"

He beat and stomped and battled each outbreak until it turned back toward the charred landscape and died. His flesh reddened and then blistered, but in spite of Si's pleas, Jake wouldn't give up.

"You've done enough harm already!" Jake screamed as he looked at the firestorm eating the dog-run, engulfing the coops and pens. Memories were vanishing before his eyes, and he was determined to put an end to that demon fire.

One man could delay a grass fire, but he couldn't stop it. Jake found himself forced back by a fresh outbreak. Only when Colonel Duncan rode up with Lute, Nathaniel, and Jefferson did the fire lose its momentum. Chris Anders rushed over a few minutes later with a handful of buckets, and Frank Selwyn arrived with the boys a quarter hour after that. Others came, too, for it was in everyone's interest to halt that fire early. With a line of men hurrying buckets of water from the creek to the fire, the flames began to lose ground. Slowly but surely Jake and his companions turned it back onto itself. Flames raced toward a final square of prairie, swallowed it, and gradually died out.

"We did it, Jake!" Si exclaimed as he slapped Jake's bare, blistered back.

"Just look at him!" Nathaniel said, laughing. "Went and changed color."

Jake was too weary to enjoy the humor being piled on him. He stumbled to the creek and collapsed in the shallows, allowing the cool water to soothe his tormented flesh.

"Jake?" Josh called, hurrying over and splashing into the creek beside him. "You've gone and burned yourself raw."

"See if you can find the wagon, Si," Frank Selwyn instructed.

"It's burned proper," Colonel Duncan explained. "Mules and all."

"Barn and house're both gone," Jake muttered. "Tried to save 'em, but—"

"I'd say you did well enough," the colonel declared.

"Saved my farm at the least," Selwyn added. "Maybe half the county."

"You can put him on my horse," Lute suggested. "Those burns need tending."

"Thanks," Si said, helping Jake to his feet. Lute brought the horse over, and the two of them swung Jake up into the saddle.

"Josh?" Jake asked. His vision began to blur, and for the first time pain erupted across his scorched back.

"We'll get you to the house," Si declared, leading Lute's horse along the creek. "Becky'll know what to do."

15

Jake had only a sketchy memory of what happened that afternoon and evening. He recalled arriving at the Selwyn place clearly enough, and after that he'd lain in a tub for a time. But when he blinked his eyes awake that next morning, he couldn't quite figure how he'd come to rest on Josh and Jordy's slat bed. Nor could he remember anyone wrapping his arms and legs in clean linen or scrubbing the smoke and grime out of his hide.

"You were a sight!" Josh said, sitting on the corner of the bed. "Black as charcoal, except for the blisters on your back."

"As I recall, you were a little smoky your-self," Jake countered.

"Didn't have half the hair burned off my head!"

"What?" Jake asked, painfully raising his arm so he could touch his fingers to his scalp. Sure enough, there wasn't much more than stubble along the left side.

"Jer volunteered to give you a haircut," Josh added. "Trim up the other side and all."

"Nice of him," Jake noted. "Had a lot of prac-tice at it, has he?"

"Lately," Josh answered. "He scalped me proper the first time, but now he's got a big bowl he plops down over my head, and trims up everything that sticks out."

"Is Si all right? Jer and Jordy?"

"Oh, they're just fine," Josh insisted. "Took us some time to get Si scrubbed white, too, but he wasn't all burned up. He and Mr. Selwyn rode out to see if they could save anything off the house and barn. Jer and Jordy went on to school."

"Not you?"

"I'm ahead on my lessons, Jake. Teacher says I'm her best pupil. I didn't figure it would hurt me to stay, and Miz Selwyn was pretty worn down last night. I thought I'd spell her and look after you."

"And the little ones?" Jake asked.

"Well, I'm not equipped to feed a baby, Jake," Josh said, grinning bashfully. "Miz Selwyn still has to tend Joel."

"So she hasn't found much rest."

"Guess not," Josh admitted. "I guess I mostly wanted to watch over you myself. I remember all those times you took care of me when I was sick. Seems only fair to return the favor."

"I'm grateful, Peanut."

"You got some visitors, too, Jake."

"Oh?"

"Colonel Duncan," Josh explained. "Skinny fellow name of Lute Gaines."

"They're here now?" Jake asked.

"Waiting on the porch. Didn't want you getting up early just to see 'em. Ready for 'em?"

"I'm not in my Sunday best, but I suppose they've seen me worse."

"After yesterday, nigh on everybody has," Josh said, laughing. "I'll fetch 'em."

Lute entered first. For a moment he stood there, frowning, but Jake waved toward a nearby chair.

"You look like something's chewed on you," Lute said, mustering a faint grin.

"No, I just got burned up a little," Jake told him. "I'd say to look at all these bandages, must've been a regiment of docs went after me."

"Just Miz Selwyn," Lute explained. "I'm afraid you got to blame me for your haircut. She told me to cut away what got singed, and all I had was shears to do it with. I expect you'll want to shoot me a time or two when you see what you look like."

"You loaned me your horse, Lute," Jake said, easing himself into a sitting position. "I figure we're even."

"Yeah, but you haven't seen your hair proper yet."

Jake laughed louder, and Lute brightened some. Colonel Duncan stepped into the room with Josh, though, and Lute turned solemn. Instantly he gave up his chair, and the colonel sat down.

"Let's go fetch Jake some of that mint tea Miz Selwyn brewed up, Josh," Lute suggested, and they hurried along outside.

"Wasn't sure you'd want to see me," the colonel said. "I judge you think me a hard man after the horse auction."

"Maybe," Jake admitted.

"You figured I owed you that stallion, Jake. In another year I'd have turned him over to you without blinking an eye."

"Another year?"

"I've had some setbacks, son," the colonel explained. "I wouldn't tell another man on earth what I'm saying to you. I lost my two best freight contracts, and that's pure put me out of business. I barely cleared enough off those horses to pay the taxes on the station. When I talked to you about your pa's debts, it was a man with experience speaking. I'm in a tight place these days."

"You could've told me," Jake declared.

"Jacob Henry, I can barely tell you now. I haven't explained any of this to Miranda. It's pride, I suppose, that keeps a man's business personal, but I don't consider that a bad thing."

"No, sir."

"I came over to tell you I appreciate the job

you did for me, and to make sure you were mending."

"I appreciate it, Colonel. I'm feeling fair."

"You take some time and heal proper, Jake, but if you're up to a ride by next week, I plan to get an outfit together."

"More mustanging?" Jake asked.

"Maybe," the colonel replied. "Mostly I'm headed west to do some ranching. The army's built a fort up on the Brazos, and I figure it's safe enough to run cattle in that country. I own close to thirty thousand acres there. I hope to round up a few hundred head and drive them into Dallas. Longhorns are thick past Weatherford, and you can get ten dollars a head for 'em once you drive 'em to market."

"Better'n horses almost," Jake observed.

"Nowhere near as tough to handle, and they don't have to be broken to saddle. A hundred head would pay my bills and give each of the hands a handsome return on their time."

"Ten dollars?" Jake asked.

"How does fifty sound?" Duncan asked. "A dollar a head bonus on any past a hundred we manage to sell."

"How many of us would there be?" Jake asked.

"Lute and Tom Carmichael are coming. Casper. The Sanderson boy from McKinney."

"Be just seven of us," Jake noted. "Pretty thin."

"Thinner without you," the colonel said. "It wouldn't be the best bargain you've ever made if you went and signed on, Jake. If you'd rather work the station, I could ask Nathaniel along. Rather have him and Jefferson together. Slaves have run away out west, and though I trust those boys to a point, it would be a considerable temptation."

"You plan to sweep up some cattle and ride home, Colonel, or is this a real ranch you plan to start?"

"I need the money now," Duncan explained. "But if we do all right, I expect to build up the place so that next spring we'll be driving longhorns north, up the Texas Road to St. Louis."

"Might turn a better profit up there on Texas cows."

"I judge it's the future for all of us, son," Duncan predicted. "We're long on cattle here, and the north's hungry. Good mix as I see it."

"I'll come, Colonel," Jake declared. "Fifty dollars and bonus, huh? What about any horses we run down?"

"What about 'em?"

"I'd say they belong to the man that ropes 'em," Jake suggested. "That way we could each of us manage a little profit off to the side."

"All right, just so long as you don't neglect your obligation to me."

"I won't, Colonel," Jake insisted.

"Get yourself well, then," Duncan urged. He rose and turned toward the door. "I'm real glad to have you with me, Jake. I appreciate you giving me this chance."

"Sir?"

"To make up for your disappointment in McKinney."

"It's already forgotten, Colonel."

"Or forgiven anyway," Duncan observed. "Thanks, Jake. See you again shortly."

Once John Duncan had left, Lute and Josh returned with a glass of mint tea. Jake sipped the cool liquid and listened to Lute blow a tune on his mouth organ.

"I guess you're going along, eh?" Josh whispered.

"Seems like a good enough notion," Jake answered.

"Jer was talking to Mr. Selwyn about you and he farming the old place on shares."

"Jer should finish his schooling," Jake declared. "Anyhow, I'm no kind of farmer. I can't even get a roof patched without the barn burning down."

"Now that was Si's fault," the eleven-year-old argued. "Everybody knows you run backward three times around a barn to get rid of an owl curse!"

Jake grinned, and little Josh chuckled.

"Peanut, one of these days we'll all of us head up to Missouri and make our fortune driving cows.

"Sure, Jake," Josh agreed. "We'll be rich."

"It isn't impossible," Jake insisted.

"What is?" Josh asked.

"Well, I don't expect to see a mule fly anytime soon," Lute said as he set aside his harmonica.

"Just as well," Josh noted. "You wouldn't want to be hit with mule droppings!"

They shared a brief laugh. Then Lute resumed his music, and Jake lay back and closed his eyes.

· · ·

Jake Wetherby had a talent for rapid healing, and under Rebecca Selwyn's care his burns improved daily. If he wasn't running around like Josh or Jordy, he was able to pitch in with the chores and oversee his brothers' lessons.

"We were hoping you would stay and work your father's place," Frank Selwyn said when Jake announced his intention to leave.

"We could work the land on shares," Jericho explained.

"Pa never made a crop worth mentioning," Jake pointed out. "Anyhow, I'm no farmer. I haven't got a talent for working the soil, nor the patience, either. Jer should finish his schooling. He's got the makings of something better."

"And you?" Jericho asked his older brother.

"I kind of like this notion of running cattle," Jake explained. "You got no big investment to make, and if it turns out we can sell 'em in Dallas like the colonel thinks, I'd say there's a real future in it. He's talked of driving a herd to Missouri, too. That sounds like a regular adventure."

"So did mustanging," Rebecca said, frowning.

"Could be I'll wind up disappointed this time, too," Jake admitted. "I know I've got some growing to do, though, and there's no place like the wilds to do it."

"There's a reason why others haven't tried this," Selwyn told Jake. "There are Comanches

161

and Kiowas up that way ready to kill any white man that rides north of the Trinity."

"Colonel Duncan says the cavalry's moved forts into that country," Jake argued.

"I never saw a cavalry outfit worth feeding," Selwyn muttered. "Mostly drunks and misfits. It takes Rangers to chase Comanches, and even they have their share of trouble. What will a half-dozen boys and an old man do if they come up against a band of raiders?"

"Most likely run," Jake answered, grinning. "I know there's a risk, Mr. Selwyn, but isn't everything? I had a little brother drown in a river, and Pa caught a chill building a dam. There just aren't any certainties out here. All a man can do is stand tall and look his friends in the eye. Hope and pray for the best."

"Well said," Selwyn noted. "Godspeed, Jake."

"We'll be praying for you, Jacob," Rebecca added.

Two days hence, after Jericho trimmed Jake's hair and Rebecca Selwyn provided some badly needed trousers and a fresh shirt, Jake rode out to Duncan's Station. Two shaggyhaired redheads greeted him at the corral.

"You must be Jake Wetherby," the oldest, a twenty-year-old scarecrow, said, extending his hand. "I'm Aaron Sanderson."

"Saw you at the auction, I believe," Jake said, gripping Aaron's wrist.

"I'm Alex," a slightly younger version of Aaron explained as he stepped over. "You were biddin' on that stallion. Shame to lose that horse."

"Oh, I've got my mare there," Jake explained, pointing to Maizy. "She gets me where I want to go."

"Can never have too many horses," Alex insisted. "But the price was a hair too high, if you ask me."

"Too high for me anyhow," Jake said, shaking Alex's hand. Jake then walked over to the station house and stepped inside. He barely had a chance to nod to Miranda before her father ordered him back outside.

"Jake's here, boys!" the colonel shouted. "Let's get ourselves mounted. We've got some riding to do."

They were four days working their way westward across northern Tarrant and Parker counties toward the Brazos River. When they passed Homer Spence's place west of the little market town of Weatherford, Jake bit his lip and urged Maizy into a gallop.

"When we're finished here, you'll have enough cash money to go and buy ol' Demon," Casper Winfrey told Jake.

"No," Lute declared. "We'll find some better horses out here. Rope one or two and gentle 'em. That Spence fellow's likely ridden all the mean off Demon by now."

"No, not that fellow," Jake argued. "He didn't look the sort to handle a horse all that well. More likely Spence is laid up with a cracked hip."

"Could be," Lute said, laughing at the notion. He then took out his mouth organ and played a bawdy tune about rye whiskey. Jake laughed and rode onward.

Colonel Duncan finally led his little band to a small clapboard trading post on the Brazos River.

"We're here," the colonel announced as he dismounted and tied his horse to a juniper sapling. "This is Baker's Trading Post. It's as close to civilization as you'll find in Palo Pinto County."

"Isn't there a county seat?" Jake asked. "Some kind of town?"

"Hasn't even been a county before this year," Duncan explained. "And it's really not organized yet."

"Then how do you know where your land is?" Jake asked. "You need a survey, don't you?"

"I don't plan to build roads nor put up a fancy house," the colonel said, laughing. "My papers locate the place between two bends of the river. I aim to verify which ones with ol' Baker here. You boys, meanwhile, best take advantage of Joe's generous hospitality. Won't find any north of here."

"Not shy of Kansas anyhow," Casper grumbled.

"Rye whiskey," Lute sang, laughing. "I can smell it from here."

"You've got a lot of experience drinking, have you?" Casper asked, grinning. "Ol' Baker don't sell anything better'n corn liquor, and it's of a quality to burn out your insides and leave your eyes crossed for a week."

"Now that's enough to tempt a Baptist," Aaron Sanderson declared as he pushed past Jake and hurried into the ramshackle trading post.

"Coming?" Tommy asked, pausing when Jake lingered outside.

"Shouldn't somebody watch the horses?" Jake asked.

"Probably," Tommy answered, "but I judge it won't be us. Come on, Jake. Best to have a sip in here. Have to last you till we have those cows rounded up and branded. And I don't figure even a Texan can get through all that without a taste of corn."

Jake nodded and stumbled along inside.

16

There wasn't a one of them glad to have visited Baker's place that next morning. Jake's head buzzed as if a thousand wasps had flown in his ear and been unable to find the way out.

"Rye whiskey," Lute managed to whine. "Sure ain't like that poison Joe Baker sells."

Jake would have laughed, but his head hurt too much. Instead he managed to climb atop Maizy and steady himself in the saddle.

"It's time to head on, boys!" Colonel Duncan shouted. He was immediately sorry to have raised his voice. The Sandersons howled a curse, and even old Casper growled.

"Sure hope there's not any Comanches up this way," Tommy said as he mounted his horse and guided two pack mules along. "We'd make a poor showing, I'm afraid."

"Hard to shoot Indians when you can't see your nose," Lute observed.

"Best shake out the cobwebs," the colonel advised. "This is just the beginning of the hard country."

Jake judged he'd never heard anything half as true. As they followed the river north and west, all hints of the gentle, rolling landscape gave way to boulder-strewn hills and flattopped mountains. The mere look of the place was hostile. To a Tennessee boy, it might as well have been the surface of the moon.

"I never saw a land so perfect for an ambush," Tommy grumbled. "You could hide a thousand Indians up one of these ravines, and a scout sitting atop those hills yonder could see us coming ten miles away!"

"Getting worried, are you, Tom?" Colonel Duncan asked.

"Colonel, I was born worried," Tommy replied. "I'm not seeing anything here to change that."

"Look over there, then," the colonel suggested, waving his hand toward a dozen longhorns grazing on buffalo grass near the river.

"There's cattle here, all right," Casper agreed. "I've run down horses in these hills, too. Shot buffalo. But as to staying long, I'd as soon shave myself with an ax. Blindfolded!"

Jake tried not to laugh at the notion, but he couldn't hold back. Afterward his head rang worse than ever.

"This is the second bend here," Duncan announced. "My land starts at the next one."

"Might be wise to keep your rifle at the ready hereafter," Tommy told Jake as he rode along the line. "Colonel, you hold on to these pack mules and I'll go have a look ahead."

"Go ahead on," Duncan said, taking charge of the animals. Tommy kicked his horse into a gallop and charged ahead. There was a fair distance between the bends, and Jake held his breath when Tommy vanished from view. The ex-cavalryman returned shortly, though, waving enthusiastically.

"You got good instincts, Colonel!" Tommy called. "Little creek cuts into the rock there. Fine place for a cabin."

"Good," Duncan declared, urging his horse onward. "Let's have ourselves a look."

"Jake?" Lute called, turning to his companion.

"Let's go," Jake answered, urging Maizy ahead. In spite of the jarring motion caused by the brief run, Jake kept up. He wasn't about to be left behind—alone.

Tommy Carmichael was right about the site. It was ideal. A rock wall of sorts protected the west bank of a winding creek. There were fifty to a hundred yards of flat country there, with good stands of live oak and willow to provide fuel and shelter. More to their purpose, the opposite bank offered a sort of natural corral for animals, what with a bluff dropping off into the Brazos swinging around in a U shape around the creek.

"That'll be our holding pen," Colonel Duncan explained. "First thing to do's string up canvas and make a work camp here. Then we'll see where the cattle are."

"I'd guess they're everywhere," Lute said, touching his toe to a cow chip. "Yonder there's horse leavings, too."

"First we worry about the cattle," the colonel insisted. "Then, if there's time, we can run in some ponies."

"Takes time to work horses, though," Lute argued. "We could be breaking 'em while we drive the cattle in."

"Sure," Jake agreed.

"What's certain is that neither of you's ever worked cattle," Duncan said, frowning. "You try it a week or so and see how much time you've got left over for mustanging."

"He's right," Casper said, laughing. "It's work that grinds you down, youngsters. And it won't wait for anything."

"No, it won't," the colonel said, tying the pack animals to a scrub oak. "Let's unpack our belongings and get to it."

The cattle roundup proved to be every bit as exhausting as Casper had warned. Even without a pounding head, the long hours of picking longhorns out of ravines and driving them to the river would have taxed Jake considerably. As it was, he was near blinded and choked by dust and tormented by his swollen head. And if all that wasn't bad enough, there was the smell.

"It's not roses, is it?" Lute asked as he pinched his nose.

"Worse'n hogs," Jake noted. "Chickens even."

"Just look on them critters as ten-dollar gold pieces," Lute suggested.

Jake tried, but it didn't help. Longhorns were generally contrary, and particularly vexing at times. He'd become adept enough at roping horses, but throwing a loop over a bull with two and a half feet of horn on either side of its head was beyond his skill. Most times he got the animals headed in the right direction by slapping their rumps with a rope's end or hollering. Maizy was becoming an accomplished herder, and she nimbly cut off rebellious longhorns while dancing away from their dangerous horns.

Jake himself had a near fatal encounter with a bull when the colonel started branding the animals with his Bar JD. Normally the Sanderson boys roped fore and hind legs, forcing an animal onto its side. Casper or the colonel then approached cautiously from the rear and pressed the white-hot iron into the animal's rump.

"Seems like it'd be better to control the horns," Lute observed.

"This is workin', ain't it?" Aaron cried. "You figure to do better, have yourself a try."

Lute took a rope and lassoed a large bull by the horns. Unfortunately, Alex was a trifle slow reacting, and before the bull could be taken down, it made a run past Lute, dragging him a dozen yards, then breaking away. Jake glanced up to find himself directly in the path of the infuriated beast.

"Lord Almighty!" Casper shouted. "Get out of there, Jake!"

The words were wasted. Jake was already racing for his life toward a nearby live oak. He jumped into the lower branches and managed to scramble higher only an instant before the bull butted the oak with all its strength. The tree rocked, and Jake was close to dislodged from his perch.

Fortunately, oak wasn't a wood easily battered. Indeed, the bull staggered back, dazed.

"Hang on, Jake!" Tommy urged as he galloped toward the live oak. He halted only long enough for Jake to drop down onto the back of the horse before racing off again.

"Ready to have another try at that bull?" Alex asked as Lute dug himself out of the dust.

"You two go ahead and do it your way," Lute said, dusting himself off. "I'm going back out to round up some cows."

They all had a good laugh at Lute's failure. As for the bull, he was beyond controlling. Tommy finally had to shoot the beast.

"Did provide a satisfying supper, wouldn't you say?" Jake asked Lute when they finished devouring roasted ribs.

"I'd say so," Lute agreed. "Sure wouldn't have cared to try and get that ornery ol' bull to town."

"No, he'd tear a peaceful little place like Weatherford to pieces," Jake declared.

Later, as the days stretched into endless torments of dust and sweat broken only by an occasional thunderstorm, Jake thought a rogue longhorn would have been a welcome change from the drudgery. Instead the outfit was plagued by rattlesnakes and scorpions. Nights were afflicted with flocks of mosquitoes as big as hornets. The only refuge from any of it was an occasional dip in the Brazos, and there, like as not, you'd find yourself chased by a cottonmouth.

All that was but a prelude to true terror, though. They had been camped on the Brazos close to two weeks with nary a sign of Indians. Twice, eight-man cavalry patrols had passed by, and Jake considered the soldiers had surely persuaded the Comanches to take their raiding elsewhere. As it happened, it wasn't Comanches who came.

Jake and Lute were sitting beside the dying embers of the evening cook fire, scraping plates while the Sandersons and Tommy enjoyed a twilight swim. Colonel Duncan had taken to his blankets early, leaving Casper to keep a loose watch over the herd. It seemed like any other night. Then all hell broke loose.

First Casper came racing across the creek, waving his hat and shouting so furiously Jake couldn't make out the words.

Lute did, though. He flung aside his plates, raced over to his rifle, grabbed it, and took shelter behind a boulder. Jake, who didn't quite understand what was happening, nevertheless followed his friend's example. Casper raced on past and beckoned the swimmers from the river. By the time they had stepped out onto the bank, a thick cloud of dust was rolling up the creek.

"Kiowas," Lute said, pointing to a couple of figures emerging from the dust swirls.

171

"They'll get the horses," Jake said, staring at Maizy, grazing restlessly a dozen yards away.

"Better the horses than us," Lute argued, but Jake wasn't having it. He hugged his Sharps and rushed out into the creek, yelling and waving his hands. Maizy instantly took flight, along with three of the others. The rest turned and galloped off right into the Kiowas.

"Jake!" Lute shouted angrily. "There goes my pony!"

"Sorry," Jake muttered as he scrambled to cover. "Want me to try and chase him down?"

Lute gazed at him with wide eyes and shook his head in disbelief.

"They're stopping," Jake observed.

"Only long enough to collect our horses," Lute noted angrily. One of the Kiowas stood out from the rest, and Lute fired at him. The shot neatly sliced one of the Indian's twin braids just below the left ear, and the startled raider turned toward the cowering cattlemen. By then Tommy and the Sandersons had managed to crawl to their blankets and pull out rifles. It was a strange sight, those three, still naked and dripping wet, taking aim on the raiders.

"You three are likely safe," Lute told them. "Ain't likely Kiowas can tell one naked fellow from another, and they'll surely think you're a brother or cousin."

"Not those Sandersons," Jake argued. "Hair's too red, and their skin's whiter'n clouds on a summer day."

"Tommy might pass," Lute said, grinning at the ex-cavalryman.

"You keep your eyes on those Indians!" the colonel demanded as he made his way around the camp. "Tom, you come along with me. There's a pair of them trying to climb the rocks and get around behind us."

"Won't try it twice," Tommy vowed, pausing only long enough to pull on a pair of trousers.

Jake watched for a few minutes as Colonel Duncan and Tommy Carmichael worked their way up the slope. Then they opened up on two shadowy figures skirting the slope. One fell like a rock. The second screamed out in pain, but he managed to limp back to cover.

"Now they'll come at us head on," Casper declared.

Jake concentrated on the narrow stretch of ground between the creek and the hillside, but the Kiowas came instead from the creek itself, using the milling longhorns to hide their initial approach. Five horsemen led the first charge, and Casper dropped the middle one with his first shot. The Sandersons, too, opened fire, and one of their bullets struck the last man on the left's horse. The three who continued on closed the distance with incredible speed. Lute waited for them to reach the bank before firing. His shot was wide, though.

Jake waited a second longer before squeezing his trigger. By then he could clearly see the Kiowa's blazing eyes and painted face. The big Sharps ball shattered the man's jaw and tore on through the back of his head, killing him instantly.

As Jake fought to reload, the two surviving Kiowas galloped toward Maizy. Casper got a shot off which dissuaded one of them, but the other managed to throw a loop over the speckled mare and drag her along.

"No!" Jake shouted, stepping out and taking careful aim. He fired, and the ball knocked the raider off his horse and into the creek. Jake raced over and drove both Maizy and the Kiowa's pony back down the creek. The Kiowa was only wounded, though. He turned and gripped a knife as he staggered toward Jake.

"Come on!" Jake shouted, swinging the rifle like a club. His eyes glowed fiercely and his heart beat furiously. The Kiowa hesitated a moment, then retreated. Jake worked to reload, but when he turned back toward the fleeing enemy, he saw a boy no older than Jericho, with blood already flowing from a deep wound in his side.

Go on, Jake silently told him. Get clear of this place and leave us be. The raider managed only three steps, though, before collapsing in the shallows.

The other Kiowas gathered the horses they had managed to capture, and their leader rode out to shout a challenge.

"You come on down here closer, and I'll put a ball in your brain, friend!" Tommy replied.

"Let 'em scream and holler," Casper advised. "Nobody's ever been killed by words."

"No," Lute agreed, turning to Jake. "There's

a couple of 'em been shot dead enough by that rifle of yours, though."

"Sure," Jake said, trembling as he gazed out at the corpses lying on the creek bank.

"You did a fair job of 'em" Tommy said as he stepped over and peered up from the rocks. "You watch those Kiowas there, Jake. They make another run at us, drop one."

Tommy, meanwhile, crept out to examine the bodies. He poked and kicked until he was satisfied they were dead. A third farther on managed to stagger to his feet, but Tommy shot him dead with a pistol.

"What're they doing?" Tommy called as he took a pouch from the second body and started back.

"Nothing," Jake answered. "Watching. Waiting."

"Can't harm us much that way," Tommy declared as he trotted back to cover. "Here, Jake. Brought you a souvenir."

"I don't want it," Jake said, ignoring the pouch.

"It's nice beadwork," Tommy argued. "Make a proper present for Miranda."

"Sure," Jake replied. "I'll tell her I took it off a Kiowa I shot."

"They were after our horses, Jake." Tommy said, staring deeply into Jake's eyes. "A man defends his property. And his friends. If he won't, he doesn't deserve either."

"I shot 'em, didn't I?" Jake cried. "You don't want me to stand up and boast about it, do you?"

"I don't understand," Lute muttered. "You did fine, Jake."

"Fine?" Jake asked, running his eyes. "I don't feel too fine."

"This is crazy," Lute complained.

"You ever kill anybody?" Tommy asked Lute. Lute gazed at his feet, and Tommy offered Jake a comforting squeeze of the shoulder. "Hits you like this sometimes, Jake. Hard. Sudden. It's not easy when you've been taught killing's sinful."

"It's not that, exactly," Jake mumbled. "It's... they were so close."

"You saw 'em good, eh?" Tommy asked. "Easier to kill somebody far off, when you don't see 'em too well. It's all the same in the end. You think on this. What would have happened if you hadn't fired? Lute there, or maybe you yourself, would likely be lying there instead. Split open like ol' Ed Raymond."

"They were only boys," Jake said, shuddering.

"They were young, all right, but the one I took the pouch off had a yellow-haired scalp tied to his rifle," Tommy explained. "So you'll excuse me for not crying over him. I've fought these people, and I don't bear 'em any particular grudge. No point to that. They'll kill you, though. It's all you have to remember. You shoot 'em before they finish you."

"One other thing," Colonel Duncan added as he joined them. "I never knew Kiowas to settle for a few horses when there were more to be had. They're sure to return."

17

Colonel Duncan took precautions against the Kiowas. Even though the outfit continued its weary roundup and branding of longhorns, at least one man stood watch with a rifle. Two men stood guard in shifts throughout the night, and the slightest sound brought the whole crew to its feet.

Jake had the midnight watch that first night. He stood at one end of the camp while Alex Sanderson prowled the opposite side. It was one of those terribly silent May nights, and the air clung to Jake's skin like a wet blanket. As he scanned the darkness, clutching the Sharps in both hands, he silently prayed the Indians had found someone else to haunt. In the distance a wolf howled eerily. The sound carried down the bluffs lining the river and echoed over and over.

"Sure," Jake whispered. "I know. You're mourning those dead boys, too."

As if hearing, the wolf grew strangely silent for a time.

"Tommy says they were killers, you know," Jake continued. "I guess you got to admit they were horse stealers anyway. But it was no different for them than chopping wood is for me. They just had a bad turn of luck. It's a heartless world, I suppose. Kills off too many good people. Ma? She never had a hard word for anybody that didn't earn it. Pa? If he wasn't sensible, at least he tried. Jeremiah? He was too little to do much wrong, and the twins hardly got themselves born!"

Jake sighed. That Brazos country was so immense, so empty. A solitary man seemed no bigger than an ant there. The wolf resumed his howling, and Jake felt tempted to join him. Somebody ought to howl at the unfairness of it all.

Two, three hours Jake kept watch. He never had quite heard what the watch was, but it seemed to stretch into days. Alex had the colonel's timepiece, and it was he who woke his brother and Lute.

"I come to spell you, Jake," Lute called from the camp. "Don't go and shoot me now."

"Try not to," Jake replied. In truth, the sound of Lute's voice had startled him considerably. Announcing himself had been a wise precaution.

"Get some rest," Lute urged as Jake yielded his sentry post. "We've got a fair amount of work left."

"Sure," Jake agreed. Colonel Duncan had suggested roping some mustangs to replace the stolen horses. He'd also insisted on waiting until five hundred cattle were branded before heading east.

"You know, we'll be lucky not to be scalped out here," Lute whispered. "All of us. If I thought a single man had a chance to get to Weatherford in one piece, I'd ride out tomorrow."

"On what?" Jake asked. "You're shy a horse."

"Fair argument," Lute observed. "Don't suppose you'd lend me Maizy."

"Not likely," Jake said, laughing. "I went and killed two Kiowas to keep her."

"So stealing her'd be risky."

"I'd say so."

"Get on to sleep, Jake," Lute urged a second time. "Wouldn't do to have a bloodthirsty fellow like you too tired to tell a friend from a Kiowa."

Jake nodded and hurried to his blankets. The wolf continued howling, but soon Jake became deaf to the sound. Fatigue had overtaken him.

Morning broke across the Brazos in an explosion of orange and scarlet. A layer of thin, wispy clouds marked the eastern horizon, and the sun drove brilliant amber spikes in a colorful fan from the distant hills.

"It's close to beautiful," Lute observed as he pulled on his britches.

"I would've said so once," Jake replied as he rubbed the mist from his eyes. "Now it looks to me like the whole world's been painted blood red."

Jake's disposition wasn't improved when the colonel passed out tins of cold beans for breakfast, either.

"We won't be wasting a lot of time cooking nowadays," Duncan declared. "Casper, you take young Lute and Jake out and see if you can scare up some horses for us. You Sanderson boys get on with the branding. Tom, you and I'll keep watch."

No one responded with much more than a grunt, and the colonel gave them all a hard stare. It was wasted. Every eye glanced up from time to time and scanned the creek. Those Kiowas weren't going far from anybody's thoughts.

Later, riding off across the low hills north of the river, Jake began to relax. He was glad to be free of cow smell and Kiowa ghosts. Tommy had dragged the corpses off and buried them in a shallow trench, but there was no erasing their youthful faces and haunting eyes from Jake's memory. He welcomed the opportunity to put some miles between them and himself.

"There's sign there," Lute called, pointing to tracks in the sandy earth near a small creek.

"Let's go slow now, boys," Casper advised. "Don't know what we're coming up on. Keep your ropes ready, but don't have your rifles too far away, either. Those ponies might just have riders."

Casper led the way on his surefooted buckskin. Jake nudged Maizy along behind. Lute brought up the rear on the colonel's sorrel. They wove their way a hundred yards along the creek before spying a dozen mustangs milling around a clearing. A boulder-crowned hill blocked their retreat. It was the perfect trap.

"Wish we had time to put up a rope fence," Casper muttered. "Things being what they are, do your best to rope one and tie it to one of those junipers. Then go after another. Be nice to grab 'em all, but we need four. Be better to have a spare or two."

"We lost the packhorses, Casper," Jake pointed out. "Don't forget them."

"We've eaten most of what was on 'em," Casper grumbled. "I don't much care whether we haul a few skillets back or not."

"Let's get at it, then," Jake suggested, and they started forward slowly. The mustangs stirred as they smelled the riders' approach, but Casper dropped a loop over a spotted stallion, and Jake roped a buckskin mare before either had a chance to react. Lute took three tries to lasso a brown mare, and by that time Casper and Jake had tied off their first ponies and captured a second. It surprised Jake to find the horses still standing around, but he soon discovered why they weren't concerned. Roping a mustang was one thing. Driving it where you wanted it was a whole other thing.

Casper suggested each of them try to lead two ponies along by their ropes while driving the remaining horses up the creek toward the cattle camp. It didn't work. The captive ponies fought the ropes, and one of Lute's broke away. Jake had the buckskin mare secure enough, but his second horse was a black stallion with a white rump. It twisted its rope and ran ahead, nearly taking Jake's head along with it. He ducked quickly, and the mare chose that moment to make her break. Maizy twisted and turned as Jake tried to hold on, but in the end the two mustangs were too much. Each broke free and Jake was thrown into the creek.

He rose, wet and angry, to find the horses trotting along south—directly toward the river and the cattle camp. Jake climbed back atop Maizy and galloped ahead. He was soon able to cut off not only the two roped ponies but several other horses as well.

"Yahhh!" he shouted, slapping his soggy hat against his knee. "Yahhh!"

The mustangs took wing, and he raced along behind, shouting and driving them toward the river. He was nearly within sight of the grazing longhorns when he realized he had lost sight of Lute and Casper.

"Lord!" Jake exclaimed, slowing Maizy and searching for his companions. He saw nothing. Fortunately, there were no Kiowas nearby or he would have made an easy target for them. Things being as they were, Jake decided to concentrate on the ponies and leave Casper to bring Lute along.

"Yahhh!" he yelled again. "Yahhh!" And the mustangs continued to race toward the Brazos.

Jake made quite a stir, charging down the little creek toward the river with nine ponies. Tommy and the colonel were standing in the rocks, waiting with rifles ready. The horses threw such a cloud of dust skyward that it was impossible to tell who was coming, or even why. Only the absence of Kiowa war cries saved Jake from a volley of rifle balls.

"Boy, have you gone addled?" Colonel Duncan asked when Jake pulled Maizy to a halt and tumbled from the saddle, as wet with perspiration as from his spill in the creek.

"Lost track of Casper and Lute," Jake explained. "Didn't know any other way to get the horses here."

"Well, you did that well enough," the colonel admitted. "Gave us quite a scare there for a moment, though."

"Guess so," Jake said, staring at his toes. "Sorry."

"No harm's done, is it, Colonel?" Tommy asked. "I guess you'll be breaking those ponies to saddle this afternoon by yourself, too, eh, Jake?"

"I hope Casper's coming along to do it mostly," Jake said, gazing back up the creek. A curtain of dust clothed the rocky countryside, and he could only cough and hope the others were all right.

"Look there," Tommy announced, pointing to a pair of riders emerging from the dust cloud. Casper dragged along the spotted stallion, but Lute trailed along on the colonel's weary sorrel, spitting out dust and cursing a blue streak.

"Beat us back, did you, Jake?" Lute grumbled. "Stole our horses, too."

"Lost track of you," Jake said, hanging his head. "Didn't mean to run out on you."

"Got the ponies here," Casper declared. "That's the main thing. How many you have roped, Jake?"

"Well, I didn't really have any of 'em roped, as it turned out," Jake confessed. "Yelled these nine back, though."

Casper slapped his knee and laughed loudly.

"Don't go enjoying yourself too much," the colonel scolded. "There's a lot of work waiting."

"Sure, Colonel," Casper agreed. "And no time like now to get after it."

After the trials of mustanging in Denton County, Jake expected a difficult time with the ponies, but Casper insisted this batch was different.

"I wouldn't be surprised if these were Indian ponies," Casper explained as he turned them in circles. "See? They're not shy of people like you'd expect. Bet I can climb atop 'em straight off."

Casper did, in fact, manage to climb atop the buckskin stallion. When Jake had a try at the white-rumped mustang, though, he found himself once again deposited in the creek.

"Won't work every single time," Casper observed. Jake shook an angry fist at the old mustanger.

In three days time, though, the mustangs responded well enough that Colonel Duncan sent Lute and Jake riding out to scour the ravines for more longhorns. After the challenge of breaking mustangs, Jake found the monotony of working cattle a trial. He soon was choked with dust, tormented by insects, and generally fed up with the smell of dung.

"Makes planting corn seem almost passable," Jake declared.

"No, that work's too tame for you now," Lute objected. "Now you're a regular Indian fighter and all."

"Well, I don't know I'd say that," Jake argued. "Wasn't much of a battle, after all, and those two weren't as old as you."

"Jake?" Lute asked, turning pale.

"What's the matter?" Jake asked, tensing.

"How old you figure those ones there are?"

Lute asked, pointing to three grim-faced Kiowas approaching from the opposite side of the ravine.

"Old enough," Jake said, reaching for his rifle. Before he could slide it out of its buckskin scabbard, the Kiowas spotted him. Whooping and waving bows, they started down the steep wall of the ravine.

"Jake?" Lute called.

"Ride, Lute!" Jake shouted, turning Maizy north. They abandoned the longhorns and galloped off across the broken country, praying they would reach cover before the Kiowas pulled even. A half mile from the river, though, Jake saw to his dismay another batch of Indians skirting the herd as they made their way toward the cattle camp.

"What now?" Lute cried.

"That hill there," Jake said, waving to a slight rise to their left.

Jake coaxed Maizy into extra effort. The trailing Kiowas were hot on their heels now, and Jake knew survival depended on getting to that hill first. Then, if they got down and got their rifles aimed, they had a chance.

"Come on, girl," Jake pleaded. "Not far now."

Maizy literally leaped up the rocky slope toward a line of boulders. The mare was panting with exhaustion when Jake rolled off her and pulled the Sharps from its scabbard.

"Get clear now, girl," Jake cried as he slapped Maizy toward a nest of scrub junipers. Lute was stumbling along toward the rocks already, waving his pistol toward the onrushing Kiowas.

"Ayyyy!" the first one screamed as he charged up the hill. Jake fell backward, then raised the Sharps, rammed back its hammer, and fired. The rifle exploded, shattering the Kiowa's left knee. The Indian cried in agony and tumbled to the earth, giving Jake a brief instant to drag himself behind the boulders and reload.

"Lord help us," Lute prayed as he nestled in alongside. "Jake, there must be a hundred of 'em!"

Jake gazed out in awe as two dozen raiders broke away from the main band and encircled the hill. The two who had been chasing Jake and Lute were busy dragging their companion down the hill.

"How many shots do you have for that pistol?" Jake asked as he realized he'd neglected to take his cartridge belt when he'd sent Maizy running.

"Holds six, but Casper said to leave one chamber empty," Lute explained.

"Well, you won't shoot your foot off now," Jake grumbled. "Load her up."

"Can't," Lute muttered. "Got no reloads."

"I've got three Sharps cartridges in my pocket," Jake explained. "So we've got nine shots. We'd have to be fair shots to drop twenty Kiowas with 'em."

"No way out of this one, is there?" Lute asked.

"None I can figure," Jake replied. "Best be ready. If we can't kill 'em, we can at least discourage 'em some. I hear they cut you up less if you give 'em a fair fight."

"I don't much care what they do once I'm dead," Lute said, trembling. "It's the cutting they do when you're still breathing that worries me."

Jake nodded and swung his rifle out toward the encircling Indians. Once the wounded man was clear, a short, broadfaced man wearing eagle feathers in his hair waved a painted lance and rode out in front. He pointed the lance up the hill, and the others charged.

Jake held his breath. Amid the world of dust thrown up by the Kiowa ponies, the raiders themselves were nearly invisible. Only when they leaped off their horses did they take human form, and then they were less than ten yards away.

Lute fired first. His bullet tore through a young Kiowa's eye and threw him back. Lute's second shot went wide, but a third and fourth staggered a large bare-chested warrior an instant before he hurled his lance past Jake's ear.

The first face Jake looked into was young, and he swung his rifle to the right and fired at an old, scar-faced Kiowa instead. The bullet struck the man's bare hip and sent him reeling. Then, before Jake could reload, the youngish Kiowa bounded over the boulders and landed atop Jake's chest, knocking the air from his lungs.

For an instant Jake imagined himself dead. Fortunately, the Kiowa, too, was stunned. Jake managed to turn his hips and throw the boy off to one side.

"Jake!" Lute screamed hideously as he

emptied his revolver at a crowd of raiders. Two continued on and drove Lute to the ground with their war axes.

Jake managed to rise and club the stunned boy across the forehead. He then dragged himself over to help Lute.

"Lute?" Jake whimpered as he stared at the bloody mess that had been his friend.

"That you, Jake?" Lute asked. His face had been pounded into a red pulp, and he had to spit blood to talk.

"I'm here, Lute," Jake whispered as he fought to reload his rifle.

"Can't see you, Jake," Lute said, reaching out with the two fingers that remained on his right hand.

"I'm here," Jake said, settling in close so Lute could touch his side. A deadly shower of arrows then fell on them, and Jake winced as the sharp edge of a stone point bit into his right ankle.

"Wish I had my mouth organ," Lute said as he broke off the shaft of an arrow that had pierced his side. "I'd blow 'em up a tune."

"Lute!" Jake screamed as he felt his companion's fingers lose their hold on his hip.

Another volley of arrows then sent Jake scurrying for cover. Gazing around, he was startled to see the Kiowas retreating. The arrows were fired from the base of the hill, by men on horseback.

"You haven't killed me yet, you butchers!" Jake shouted, ramming a cartridge into the Sharps and snapping a cap in place. He aimed at the lance-waving chief and fired. The rifle exploded, and its projectile knocked the Kiowa leader from his pony. The others shouted angrily, but instead of charging anew, they turned and retired to the east.

"Whhhat..." Jake stammered.

To his amazement, a long file of blue-shirted soldiers advanced on the Kiowas from the west. Their leader was a stone-faced man of medium stature who waved the column onward with a pistol. The soldiers made only a half hearted run at the Kiowas before turning back toward the hill, but Jake judged it was enough to save his life.

"Colonel, there's one of 'em still alive up here!" a bearded corporal announced as he halted his horse near the boulders where Jake was sitting beside Lute's body.

"Well, he's one fortunate young man," a voice Jake had expected to be John Duncan's observed. "Bring him down, Corporal. Bring him down."

"I can bring my own self down," Jake barked, blinking a tear from his eye and wincing from the pain in his ankle.

"Easy there, son," the corporal said, climbing off his horse and taking Jake in hand. "You got an arrow in that foot."

"Don't you figure I know it?" Jake shouted. "I've got a friend up there who's dead!"

"By the looks of it, you got some of them, too," the corporal said, lifting Jake off his feet and settling him on a nearby boulder. "Now be still a minute. We've got no surgeon with us, and I'm as good a man as the next to cut that arrow out."

Before Jake had a chance to argue, the corporal cut a slit in Jake's boot and pried the arrow from his ankle. Jake howled with pain and then collapsed.

18

When Jake regained consciousness, he found himself resting back at the cattle camp. Colonel Duncan and the cavalry commander were gabbing nearby. Tommy and some of the soldiers were turning a side of beef on a spit. Casper sat with Jake, concern etched across his face.

"Had a good rest, did you?" Casper asked when Jake blinked his eyes awake.

"My foot hurts," Jake complained.

"Had an arrow dug out of it," Casper explained. "Lucky it was Kiowas. I heard of tribes that poison their points."

"Lute..."

"Yeah," Casper said, frowning. "Had himself some bad luck. I'd like to take him along home, but the colonel says he doesn't really have one."

"Here's as good a place as another," Jake said, fighting off the memory of his friend's bloody face.

"They got the Sanderson boys, too," Casper added. They were busy branding across the creek when that pack charged us. Never had a chance. Kiowas just rode 'em down."

"I ought to be dead, too," Jake declared.

"Well, you're not altogether whole as it is," Casper pointed out. "We'd all be buzzard meat if those cavalry boys hadn't come along. Can you believe it? Colonel was tired of garrison duty, he says, so he decided to ride out and see some of the country."

"I wouldn't judge it quite as odd as that," Colonel Duncan declared as he stepped over and gave Jake a fatherly tap on the shoulder. Behind Duncan stood a tall man in a blue military uniform. "This is Colonel Robert Lee, Jake. He was quite a hero in the war with Mexico. Made a name for himself scouting the enemy then, too, and I never judged it coincidence when he chased the enemy back then. Don't now, either."

"Me and Colonel Duncan served together with the Rangers back then," Casper noted. "We didn't get on with the regular army too well most times, but I'll admit I'm glad to see 'em today."

"Me, too," Jake said, gazing over at the cavalrymen.

"I'm glad we came in time to extricate you, young man," Colonel Lee said. Jake was struck by the smooth southern drawl of the officer. Maryland or Virginia, Jake judged. It was out of place on the Texas frontier.

"Thanks for all you did," Jake said, nodding respectfully at the officer.

"Colonel Duncan, can we escort you and your men to Camp Cooper?" Colonel Lee asked. "It's rough as posts go, but I imagine it's safe from attack."

"I've got cattle to move," Duncan insisted.

"You mean to go ahead and try to drive a herd to Dallas?" Tommy asked. "Just the four of us? And Jake there lamed up?"

"You certainly don't mean for that boy to ride," the cavalry corporal grumbled.

"No point you hauling him west when we can get him to a town riding the same distance east," Duncan argued.

"I mean to finish this drive," Jake declared. "A man finishes what he starts, doesn't he, Colonel Duncan?"

"Colonel?" Casper asked wanly.

"He's got a considerable stake in this herd," Duncan growled. "Cattle and horses, too. I won't deprive him of what's due him."

"I once walked ten miles on a broken ankle," Jake boasted. "I bet I can ride fine on this one. On Maizy anyway. Where is that fool mare?"

"Growing fat on river grass," Tommy assured Jake. "Trotted right along in here like there wasn't anything happening."

"There," Duncan said, nodding. "We have four of us to see the job done."

"Well, if you're bound and determined to drive these cows east," Colonel Lee said, "I recommend you break camp at dawn. We'll stay overnight and enjoy that beef you promised. I wish I could offer escort, but we're thin out here as it is."

"You boys chase those Kiowas north," Casper suggested. "Then won't any of us need escorts."

"Now don't go getting carried away, Casper,"

192

Tommy crackled. "Wouldn't want to tame this country too fast. Got to leave something to challenge Jake here when he grows up."

"I figure he's gone and done that," Casper barked. "if he's old enough to get arrow-shot, he's old enough to count himself a man. We've buried younger ones, don't forget."

"I haven't," Tommy confessed.

And I can't, Jake thought.

That night the cattle camp filled with soldier songs. Cavalryman and cowboy alike satisfied his hunger on fresh beef and biscuits. Afterward Jake slept soundly in spite of a throbbing ankle. And next morning, even before the soldiers broke camp, Casper and Tommy were nudging the lead cows along the river.

"Guess it's up to us to bring up the rear, son," Colonel Duncan announced as he helped Jake hobble toward Maizy. "That leg gets to bothering you, holler out, won't you?"

"Sure, Colonel," Jake agreed. In truth, though, he didn't expect to say a word so long as he could remain in the saddle.

Trailing along in the dust thrown up by four hundred fifty longhorns was a poor way to earn a living, Jake quickly decided. Once the herd got moving, the colonel rode out to take the lead. Tommy and Casper rode along the left flank as they made their way along the Brazos. With the river cutting off any avenue of escape on the right, all Jake had to do was shout the spare horses and straggling cows onward.

At first Jake felt obligated to coax each

stray from a ravine or whip the animals along when they fell back.

"Colonel doesn't expect to get every one of them to market," Casper told Jake after a time. "Just keep the horses with us. We'll be needing those mounts."

"Sure," Jake agreed.

"Colonel told me he figures those ten we brought in are ours, too, Jake. We'll sell 'em and split the profit even."

"You did most of the work," Jake argued. "I'd settle for—"

"Who drove 'em in in the first place?" Casper asked. "You did the hard part. I won't argue it, either, Jake."

"You're the boss, then, Casper," Jake replied with a grin.

"See you don't forget that," Casper urged. "Especially when it means cash money to you."

Once they passed Baker's Trading Post, Duncan swung the herd due east. Jake lingered a moment at the river, remembering that Brazos River corn liquor he'd shared with Lute. Each mile now Jake began to think more and more about Lute. The music was especially missed.

"Well, you blow up a tune for Saint Peter, won't you?" Jake whispered to the wind.

Gradually they made their way east. Colonel Duncan estimated they made ten miles that first day and another fifteen the next. The third morning, they passed to the south of Weatherford, and the colonel managed to sign on a pair of extra hands for the remaining journey.

Max Schuman and Brent Wylie were seasoned hands who had been sent packing by Homer Spence the week before.

"Appears Spence spent all his cash buying your horse, Jake," Casper said, shaking his head. "Can't afford to keep on a full crew."

Jake hoped that was the reason. The newcomers clearly knew their trade, but they kept to themselves at night, and there was something odd about the way they sat by the fire, whispering. When Jake or Tommy approached, they went mute.

"I don't like 'em," Jake told Casper.

"They pull their weight, don't they?" Casper asked. "Don't hold it against 'em they signed on late."

"I never thought less of the Sandersons," Jake argued. "These two are up to something, though."

"What would they be up to?" Casper asked.

"I don't know," Jake answered. "It's just that..."

"You were right the first time," Casper scolded. "You don't know. Do your job and leave the colonel to worry over the crew."

Jake tried to do it, but that fourth night, as the outfit camped on the Trinity River in Tarrant County, he felt oddly nervous. He was supposed to share the middle watch with Wylie, but Schuman had insisted on taking it instead.

"See there, Jake?" Casper asked. "Wanted you to have some extra rest."

"Hope that's it," Jake muttered as he took to his blankets. "Smells funny to me."

Colonel Duncan didn't appear concerned,

195

though, nor did Casper and Tommy. Jake forced his suspicions into the back of his mind and tried to find some sleep.

Gunshots woke him shortly after midnight. Three horse men were exchanging shots with Tommy while Schuman and Wylie appeared to be ransacking the camp.

"Where's the money, Max?" Wylie shouted. "You said you saw the old man salt it away."

"He did," Colonel Duncan declared as he leveled a double-barrel shotgun at the two would-be thieves. "Why don't you call your friends in, boys, so we can have a talk?"

Schuman made a break toward his right, and Duncan fired one barrel. A blast of buckshot ripped Schuman apart and left him lying limp and lifeless on the ground.

"Was all his idea, Colonel!" Wylie whimpered as he hid his face.

"Call 'em in!" Duncan barked, cocking the second hammer.

"Boys!" Wylie shouted. "Come in!"

A half second later Tommy finally hit one of them. The other two turned and raced off into the darkness.

Casper, who had been minding the herd, trotted up with a length of rope while Tommy dragged a boy of fifteen or so along. The stranger cradled a shattered right arm and winced as waves of pain surged through him.

"No, sir," Wylie pleaded as he spied the rope. "You can't, Colonel. We meant you no harm."

"Just shot bullets into my bed's all," Duncan said, nodding to where his blankets lay draped over a pair of saddles.

"Cain't blame me," the wounded boy argued. "He's my uncle. I had to."

"I didn't see anybody holding a gun to your head, boy," Casper grumbled as he tossed one end of the rope over a live oak branch.

"You can't just hang 'em," Jake objected as he limped over. "They have to have a trial."

"Where?" Duncan asked. "There's no jailhouse hereabouts. I don't plan to go dragging 'em into Dallas with us, not with their two friends still out there. We've got no time for trials, Jake. And what difference would it make anyway?"

"Just doesn't seem right," Jake insisted, gazing into the eyes of his companions.

"You were the one got us thinking," Casper complained. "If you hadn't spoken up, I wouldn't have sneaked over and listened to them planning it."

"Jacob Henry," the colonel said, staring hard at Jake. "They meant to murder us all. Steal what money I had and run the herd into town as their own."

"I never knew," the wounded boy pleaded, dropping to his knees. "Please, mister, I don't even have a gun."

"That right, Tom?" Duncan asked.

"Somebody was sure shooting at me," Tommy replied.

Colonel Duncan stepped over and searched the boy.

"Nothing on him now," the colonel admitted.

"Likely dropped it when I shot him," Tommy argued. "Colonel, you know how it is. If it's right for one to hang, the other's got to swing, too."

"He's no older'n Lute," Jake objected.

"I never held it against Lute his pa was a road agent," Duncan said, sighing. "But this fellow's got more than bad blood to get him hung. He came in here tonight to steal cattle at best, and that's a capital crime anywhere I've been. Jake, I admire you for your forgiving heart, but it's wasted on these two."

"Uncle Brent, tell 'em," the boy begged. "Tell 'em you said I was just supposed to help you take some horses into Dallas."

"Hush, boy," Wylie barked. "You ain't a good liar."

"No, you're not," Tommy said as Casper fashioned a noose. "I smell powder on your clothes."

"So I had a gun," the boy said, forcing a smile on his face. "I didn't—"

"Hush," Tommy shouted. "Hush or I'll gag you. I'm tired, and I need my sleep."

"You mean to do it now?" Wylie asked. "Right now?"

"Soon as I get the other rope ready," Casper explained.

Wylie lowered his eyes. Jake thought he detected a tear in the thief's eye.

"You'll bury us at least, wont' you?" the boy asked. "Put a marker up. My name's Andy... Andrew. Andrew Wylie. Lord help me, I'm only sixteen."

"Old enough to steal," the colonel mused. "Old enough to die."

Casper threw a second rope over the oak limb and formed a noose. He then waved to Tommy, who prodded Andy Wylie toward the rope. His uncle came over on his own.

"Can't I say anything to change your mind?" Wylie asked. "Anything at all?"

"Nothing," Duncan said as he personally slipped the noose over Wylie's neck. Casper placed the second noose around young Andy's neck and satisfied himself both were tight. Tommy then took the free end and pulled hard until he had raised Wylie a foot and a half off the ground. As Tommy tied off the rope, Wylie kicked and clawed at the noose, trying to free himself as he slowly strangled.

"Shoot me," Andy pleaded. "Don't do it this way."

"Got to be," Tommy said, pulling on the second rope. At first Andy remained quiet as the rope tightened. Then he kicked out and made a slow gurgling sound. A foul odor struck Jake's nostrils, and he noticed both men had soiled themselves.

"Why, Colonel?" Jake asked.

"When you're older, son, you'll come to understand that out here the only law that counts for much is survival," Duncan said, turning away from the corpses. "Lute learned that on the Brazos. I guess maybe you're learning it now. If we'd let them go, they would have tried the same trick on somebody else. If we'd found a judge and a jury, they would only have brought 'em to this same end."

"It wouldn't have been us did it," Jake insisted.

"Sure, it would have," Casper argued. "You

think a man who bears witness in court isn't tightening a noose same as I did? Anyhow, wasn't us aimed a gun or thought to steal. The ones to blame are hanging right there. If it's a hard way to die, it's meant to be. Discourages thieves."

Jake drew out a knife and stepped toward the ropes, but Casper stopped him.

"Leave 'em," Casper said, gripping Jake's shoulders. "It's an example to those who pass by."

"But you promised—" Jake began.

"Said nothing," Casper told him.

"It's how it is out here," Tommy added. "Hard. Cruel most times. But simple in its way. You walk a straight path, and there's a hundred ways to come to an early end. You turn crooked, you add a few more."

"Understand, Jake?" Casper asked.

"No," Jake answered. "But I don't suppose it much matters. They're dead, like Lute's dead, like little Ty Raymond's dead. Seems to me that's what this country's for, hurrying boys to an early grave. Or leaving 'em hanging here so the birds can have at 'em!"

Jake turned and limped out to where the horses stood hobbled beside the Trinity. He sat there for a time, whistling a tune to Maizy. Then he lay back against a live oak and fell asleep.

19

When Jake awoke, he discovered the Wylies and Schuman had been buried beneath the hanging tree. Someone had carved their names into the tree trunk. Jake didn't know who did it, and no one admitted the deed, but he suspected Casper. There had been more than a hint of compassion in the old-timer's eyes as he'd turned Jake away from the tree.

What scant satisfaction Jake felt from the burying quickly vanished as he gazed out at the longhorns. During the night the herd had dispersed considerably. He hadn't looked forward to crossing the river with four hundred fifty cattle, and to make matters worse, they would be most of the day just rounding up strays.

"Most likely it was the gunshots," Casper grumbled as he and Jake rode out to run the strays back toward the Trinity. "Lucky we didn't have a stampede."

"Sure," Jake muttered. His ankle was hurting, and his conscience continued to plague him over the hanging of the Wylie boy. Moreover, Lute hadn't been dead a week yet.

"Can't take everything to heart," Casper advised. "Nobody ever promised you an easy ride, Jake. I never found a road that offered many comforts. Best leave the sadness behind and ride on."

"Weren't you ever young, Casper?" Jake

asked. "Death rests heavy on a young man."

"On anybody," Casper confessed. "As to being young, no, I was born old. Comes of living with horses and addlebrained wranglers."

"Sure," Jake said, forcing a faint smile onto his face. "Guess you learn to take the rough spots with the smooth."

"That's it exactly," Casper said, cutting off a reluctant cow and shouting it along. "Elsewise you strike camp then and there. I figure it pleases ol' Lute some to know you're riding into town with horses to sell and a bonus to collect. I expect your brothers'll be happy to see you, too. Know Miss Miranda will."

"Do you now?" Jake asked.

"Well, she never took half so much interest in me, I'll tell you. Frying up steak for a fellow's breakfast!"

"Where'd you hear that?" Jake asked.

"Got ears, boy, even if they're old," Casper said, laughing. "Now let's get these cows run in. I've got a thirst, and it ain't getting satisfied short of Dallas."

"Yahhh!" Jake yelled at the straggling longhorns, and Maizy raced along, urging them onward. He actually found the work took some of the sting out of his ankle, and the shouting released some of his gloom.

Colonel Duncan was satisfied that most of the herd had been reassembled that afternoon, and he decided to make the crossing before dusk darkened the land. There was a fine ford nearby, and the colonel led the first batch across himself. Afterward Jake, Tommy, and Casper had the more difficult task of coaxing the others through the shallows and on to the other side.

"I do believe a longhorn's the only critter I ever saw less eager to take to water than ol' Casper!" Tommy exclaimed.

"You don't smell so pretty yourself!" Casper answered.

The two of them shouted back and forth across a hundred swimming cattle, and Jake found himself laughing at it. Personally, he welcomed the brief dip in the Trinity. It washed the dust and sweat from his face and cooled Maizy considerably.

"Get those two on the left!" Casper called, and Jake splashed over and drove them back toward the ford.

"Fool cows!" Jake shouted. "Want to drown?"

"They're like as not to do it just to cheat us out of our bonus!" Casper complained.

"We could drown half of them and still have a hundred head," Jake pointed out. "Anyhow, the horses are our cash crop."

So he hoped anyway. Each night Jake hobbled their feet and saw they had good grass to chew and water to drink. Being range ponies, they were used to foraging for themselves, but he wasn't taking any chances. The longhorns were at least as self-reliant, after all, and Colonel Duncan rested and watered them with a father's doting eye.

"He'll pay his notes and have cash money left over," Casper noted. "You can see it in his eyes. He's already counting the bank notes."

Jake didn't comment. After all, he was doing the same thing himself.

The last three days were the slowest. Colonel Duncan kept a wary eye on strangers traveling the dusty trail between the small outlying towns and the thriving little collection of buildings that Dallas had become. What had once been a crossing on the Trinity now boasted a fine hotel, small courthouse, and two entire streets of shops and stores.

"First time I came through here, there was nothing but a couple of cabins," Casper told Jake when they drove the herd up next to the Trinity.

"We'll leave 'em here for now," Colonel Duncan said, nodding to Casper. "I'll bring the buyers out to have a look."

"When do we get to town?" Tommy asked anxiously.

"After we turn the stock over," Duncan answered. "Keep watch on 'em till then. Jake, you treat those horses good, too. You'll want to take them along into town and have an auction."

"Yes, sir," Jake replied.

"Till then, gentlemen," the colonel said, tipping his hat and rearing his sorrel up on its hind legs. He then galloped off to Dallas.

When Colonel John Duncan returned later that day, he was a changed man. He wore a new tailored suit and a broad-brimmed tan hat. His starched white shirt was decorated with a black string tie, and a fifty-cent cigar stuck out of the corner of his mouth.

With him rode three similarly attired men.

Two were ranchers and the third was a Dallas butcher.

"We flooded the market boys," Duncan explained. "Butcher Faraday won't buy but fifty. I'm selling the surplus to Tim Post there and Gil King."

Jake nodded to the men, but they didn't take notice of him. Their eyes were fixed on the long-horns. The ranchers worked their way around the herd, nodding to a bull here and a cow there.

"Good enough stock, I'd judge," Post declared. "We'll head back into town and settle on terms."

"We'll settle here and now," King insisted. "I've got a crew headed out to drive two hundred head on south. Been waiting a week already, John. Expected you earlier."

"We had some trouble, as I explained," the colonel answered. "If Tim's got no objection, we can tend to your two hundred now and leave his for later."

"I won't take seconds," Post grumbled. "We'll do it now."

"Doesn't so much matter to me if you two fight over the bulls," Faraday muttered. "I just want good sound animals with no hint of sickness. I can take 'em now or later, John, so long as your boys bring 'em along to town."

The colonel then began dickering with the buyers. Jake heard only a little of the talk, and that was disappointing. The ranchers weren't offering but eight or nine dollars a head, and the butcher bid even less.

"Price always falls when the supply's high," Casper explained. "Don't worry, Jake. We'll come out of it fine, and so will the colonel."

Sure, Jake thought. After all, there were three less men to pay.

As it turned out, King's men arrived late, and Post didn't bring his crew until the following morning. Jake wound up passing a final night on the Trinity. Early that next morning, though, he rode with Casper and Tommy through the dusty streets of Dallas with Faraday's fifty head and the horses. Most of the town came out to greet them, for there were many passing through on their way north or south, and others only freshly arrived from the east. To such folks a longhorn was a mythical creature, and fifty of them in one place was a regular event.

Once Faraday accepted delivery of the longhorns, Colonel Duncan and Tommy headed for the nearby Lone Star Saloon. Jake and Casper led their ten dusty mustangs down to the livery and corral of a fellow named Art Patrick.

"Mind if we leave these ponies here long enough to clean 'em up some?" Casper asked.

"Not so long as you don't sell 'em till I get a chance to make an offer," Patrick replied. "I'm always shy of saddle horses these days."

"We never sent a buyer away," Jake said, grinning. "Happy to hear offers."

"I'd take the whole bunch for two hundred," Patrick offered.

"Casper?" Jake asked, counting the money in his head.

"Sure, you would, friend," Casper said, grinning. "But I expect to do a hair better when word gets around town. Jake, you get 'em ready. I'll go talk 'em up and grab something to stop that belly of yours from rumbling. We'll hold an auction around one this afternoon. Fair enough?"

"Sure," Jake agreed.

He devoted the balance of the morning to cleaning and brushing the ponies. Except for a brief pause to gobble some tamales, he worked up until the auction, brushing those range ponies until their coats took a shine the equal of a Kentucky pacer's.

Casper handled the auction, but before he began, Jake led off the big stallion with the white rump.

"I guess maybe I knew you'd be keeping him," Casper said, laughing. "No Demon maybe, but he's steadier. Better feet, too. Be a sounder horse in the long run."

"You should take that buckskin for yourself," Jake advised.

"We're not helping our crop, cutting out the best two," Casper observed, "but that's the trouble with horse lovers. We take our critters too much to heart."

Jake grinned his answer. It was a backhanded compliment, sure, but high praise coming from Casper Winfrey.

The other eight found a mixed reception. Four gentlemen in need of mounts bid fairly freely, and Casper collected a hundred and fifty dollars off them. The remaining four brought in only twenty dollars each.

"Not much better than Patrick offered," Jake said as he pocketed his half.

"Can't expect too much better in a place like Dallas," Casper argued. "Anyhow, the two we kept were worth the rest combined. I've got the start of my horse ranch, you see, and the colonel's yet to pay off."

"Best we catch up with him before he buys another hat," Jake suggested.

They tied their horses to a hitching post in front of the Lone Star and stepped inside. Colonel Duncan and Tommy were seated at a corner table, sipping whiskey.

"There's the rest of our outfit now," Tommy announced, waving wildly. "Sell your ponies, did you?"

"Sure did," Jake boasted.

"Didn't do so well as we'd hoped, but I've fared poorer," Casper declared. A girl brought two fresh glasses over, and Casper poured himself a drink. Jake turned his glass over and shook his head.

"I get to Harrison's Crossroads with whiskey breath, and my sister's sure to have me baptized all over," he explained.

"Still haven't shook off that Brazos corn, eh?" Tommy whispered.

"There's that, too," Jake confessed.

"You boys ready to settle up?" Colonel Duncan asked, pulling out an envelope stuffed with bank notes.

"Seems as good a time as another," Tommy answered.

"Here's the fifty I promised you, then," Duncan said, counting out the money. "Extra twenty for Casper, he being particular expensive due to his fine manners."

Jake and Tommy grinned. Casper merely accepted the money.

"We sold four hundred twelve," Duncan added. "I promised a bonus of a dollar a head. Three hundred twelve each."

Jake gazed at the mounting pile of money with widening eyes. When the colonel stacked an extra fifty onto each pile, Jake gazed up in confusion.

"I would never've managed it without considerable extra effort on your part," Duncan explained, avoiding their eyes. "I don't come by grateful words easily, and I've been a hard man for a boss sometimes. I'm grateful you all made it through the storm, and I hope you'll take the extra fifty and have yourselves a high time on the colonel."

"Man must think highly of you, boys," Faraday remarked from the next table. "John Duncan's stingy with his money."

"And worse where high words are concerned," a saloon girl added with a grin.

"Don't mind them, Colonel," Tommy said, laughing. "As for the good time, consider it a promise," he added as he poured himself another whiskey.

"I have need of a regular outfit next week when I head back to the Brazos," Duncan added. "I'd welcome any of you. Or all."

"Take me a week to sober up from tonight," Tommy boasted. "But I'll be along."

"Got no better offer," Casper declared.

"Jake, don't you answer right away," the

colonel said, turning somber. "First I'd like to bend your ear a moment."

"Yes, sir," Jake said, rising and following Colonel Duncan outside.

For a time Duncan paced back and forth on the heavy boardwalk outside the saloon. Jake found himself staring at the raggedy remains of his clothes, at his split boot, at the spindly excuse for a man that he was.

"I understand, Colonel," Jake said, sighing. "You need real scrappers for that Brazos country, not boys sure to go soft over a hanging or turn sour when a friend gets himself killed. You've done right by me, sir. I have money to start fresh. Don't worry. I'll make out."

"I've never found any easy going, Jacob Henry," Duncan replied. "As that gal inside said, I don't find words easily come by at times."

"Sir?

"You misjudge my meaning, son," the colonel said, taking off his hat and brushing back his hair. "I wasn't intending criticism. Truth is, you surprised me."

"Figure I have the makings of a stockman, Colonel?" Jake asked.

"Guess you'll do till something better comes along," Duncan answered. "Yes, you'll do right enough."

"I can call on you next week, then?" Jake asked.

"I'd deem it a favor, Jake," the colonel added, offering his hand. "And a privilege."

20

Jake delayed his return to Harrison's Cross-roads long enough to treat himself to a hot bath, shave, and haircut at Colomby's Tonsorial Palace down the street. Afterward he outfitted himself from nose to toe in new clothes. He winced a hair at paying over twenty-five dollars, but when he gazed in a mirror afterward, he considered it worth every penny. He spent another ten buying a bolt of muslin for Jane Mary and leather hats for each of his brothers. Finally he indulged himself on a sack of stick candy.

"Guess you're not so grown as you thought, Jake," he told himself afterward.

The ride north required the balance of the day, and Jake appeared at Harrison's store as darkness settled in. Over at Doc Springfield's house he spotted Betsy and Baby Joe playing with the doc's children.

"Howdy," he called, waving.

The youngsters nodded, and Betsy stared hard. She didn't recognize him for a moment, and when she did, she smiled and gave him a nod of approval.

Jane Mary didn't have any trouble identifying him, but the shock that filled her bright blue eyes brought Jake even greater satisfaction.

"Jacob Henry?" she cried. "I don't believe it. Have you gone and gotten yourself elected governor?"

"Just a simple stockman," Jake explained as he untied the bolt of fabric from the stallion. "Gone and did all right by myself, sis."

"I'd judge so," she replied, trotting out and wrapping her arms around him. "Would you believe it? You've stretched yourself so tall I have to settle for kissing your chin."

"I never recall you being all that eager to kiss me before," he noted.

"You never smelled of lilac water before," she said, laughing. "Nor would you sit still for it."

"Well, a man can change some," Jake admitted. "You see if you can put this to some use while I tether my horses."

"Leave that to me," Martin insisted as he stepped outside. "That leg troubling you, Jake?"

"Ankle," Jake admitted. "Had an arrow cut out of it."

"What?" Jane Mary gasped.

"I'll tell you all about it," Jake promised.

"Later," she suggested. "Just now I think I'd better feed you. You're thinner, I think."

"No, I burst right out of my old clothes."

"Well, you look thin to me, Jacob Henry Wetherby, and I never knew you not eager to eat."

"Now that hasn't changed," he agreed.

Over supper he shared some particle of his adventures, toning them down so as not to worry her past reason. Afterward he drew out a new leather wallet full of bank notes.

"I thought maybe you'd look after this for me," he said soberly. "You know Pa didn't trust banks, but even that would be better than carrying folding money out onto the plain."

"You're going back?" she asked.

"Colonel Duncan's invited me, sis," he told her. "And the truth is, I'm hungry to try it again."

"Jake, there's a fortune here!" Jane Mary said as she counted up the notes. "You could buy land."

"Farm?" Jake asked, laughing. "No, sis, I think I found a place where I can belong. Who knows? If we can make a few more of these drives, maybe I can start a horse ranch. Jer should be ready for some adventure by then, and—"

"There's a lot of Joe Wetherby in you, Jake," she noted, smiling. "Dreaming big."

"Worried?"

"No, on you it looks good. Truth is, I missed the brightness you used to have. There've been too many disappointments lately. You ought to dream some."

"I won't let my feet get too far off the ground," he promised.

After breakfast that next morning, Jake saddled Maizy and rode up Spring Creek to the Selwyn place. His brothers were off at school, so after chatting awhile with Frank and Rebecca, he rode out west with Si Garrett toward the old Wetherby farm.

"It's changed a good deal," Si observed. "After the fire and all. See there how the grasses have sprung up and covered up everything?"

"New growth," Jake said, nodding. "I always

took that as a good sign, sort of a rainbow after the storm. Life going on."

"We planted the fields, and the peaches will be ripening soon. I always envied you those trees."

"Because you never picked peaches," Jake said, laughing. "But I'll admit they have a sweet taste."

"I've got some fences to look after now," Si explained when they neared the little graveyard hill. "I expect you'll have somethin' to keep you busy."

"Yes, I imagine so," Jake admitted. He then nudged Maizy to the right and climbed down. The hill was covered with colorful wildflowers, all of it but the graves themselves, which were outlined with whitewashed stones. Jake knew his brothers must be visiting the place often.

"Ma, Pa," he whispered as he knelt beside the markers, "it's Jake. Just wanted you to see I'm getting on. Got myself some size, Pa. Finally. May not be a runt after all. Ma, I miss you. And I remember the better times, Pa."

He sat there silently half an hour or so, recalling those better times. Then he rose and limped to Maizy, mounted, and rode back down the creek.

Late that afternoon, when his brothers returned from school, they led Jake to the deep pool where they'd so often swum away summer afternoons.

"Well?" Jordy asked, kicking off his shoes and wriggling out of his overalls. "You waiting on Christmas or something?"

214

Jake laughed, and his brothers hurriedly shed their clothes and splashed into the cool water. For a time the four Wetherbys swam and raced and tried to drown each other. Then Jake led them to the bank and shared his adventures.

"That where the arrow got you, eh?" Josh asked, tracing the scar with his finger.

"Lucky it didn't get you any higher," Jordy declared. "I hear they chop legs off when a fellow gets arrow-shot."

"Yes, I was properly fortunate," Jake agreed. As he told them of Lute and the hard days afterward, Josh crept closer. Jordy and Jer nodded somberly.

"You here to stay a bit, Jake?" Jordy asked at last.

"Sure, he is," Josh added. "We've got peaches to pick in a week or so. He can help."

"We'll swim some," Jake promised. "Maybe ride out and hunt a deer. Next week I'm going back to the colonel's, though."

"After all you been through?" Jordy cried. "Lord, Jake, you'll get killed this time."

"We'll find you a job," Jericho vowed.

"You don't understand," Jake told them. "Look at me. Don't you see I've changed? I'm tall enough to hold my own."

"Never considered otherwise," Jericho insisted. "We miss you though, Jake. Can't you stay?"

"Jake?" Josh pleaded.

"I miss you, too," Jake confessed. "But, well, its hard to explain."

"You wanted your adventure," Jericho observed. "Wasn't enough, I guess."

"It's more," Jake argued. "Pa found Texas inviting him out. He had to travel, just like his Pa had to come to Tennessee. Me, it's the Brazos now, and later, who knows? I'm a Wetherby, and there's new country there. It's calling."

"Sure," Jericho said, nodding. "I can almost hear it myself."

"Me, too," Jordy added with a grin.

"Even me," Josh said, resting a hand on Jake's shoulder.

"One of these days we'll have ourselves a big ranch out there," Jake said. His eyes caught fire, and as he dreamed aloud, his brothers gazed westward.

They won't stay small, Jake told himself. I grew tall. They will, too. Perhaps the vow he'd made his father wasn't past keeping.

"You know, the colonel told me next year he'll drive cattle all the way to St. Louis!" Jake announced. "Now there's an adventure worth undertaking."

"Figure he'll need some extra hands?" Jordy asked.

"Sure, he will," Jericho declared. "Now that'd be a thing worth telling your grandkids, wouldn't it? First outfit up the trail to St. Louis."

"We'll have to do some powerful growing," Josh said, gazing up at Jake with a glimmer in his eye. " 'Course, we're Wetherbys. If Jake can do it, anything's possible!"

His brothers then dragged him back into the creek and did their best to drown him.

Seeing the shine on their faces, and feeling the closeness they shared, made a few mouthfuls of creek almost worth it.

Of course the hats would wait now. At least till after supper.